THE DEVIL IS A PART-TIMER!

10

TOSHI
AGAHARA
STRATION BY
029 (ONIKU)

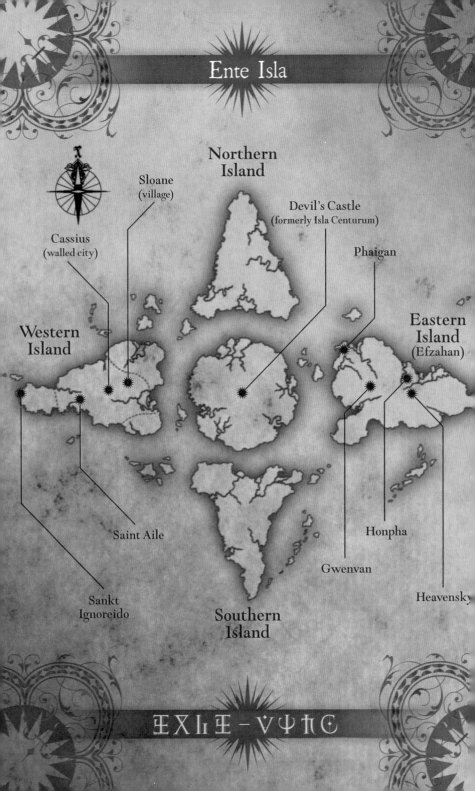

Ente Isla

Northern Island

Western Island

Eastern Island
(Efzahan)

Southern Island

Sloane
(village)

Cassius
(walled city)

Devil's Castle
(formerly Isla Centurum)

Phaigan

Saint Aile

Sankt
Ignoreido

Gwenvan

Honpha

Heavensky

Contents

Design:kimura design lab

SATOSHI WAGAHARA

ILLUSTRATED BY ■ 029 (ONIKU)

10

THE DEVIL IS A PART-TIMER!

YEN ON

NEW YORK

THE DEVIL IS A PART-TIMER!, Volume 10
SATOSHI WAGAHARA, ILLUSTRATION BY 029 (ONIKU)

Translation by Kevin Gifford
Cover art by 029 (oniku)

HATARAKU MAOUSAMA!, Volume 10
© SATOSHI WAGAHARA 2013
Edited by ASCII MEDIA WORKS
First published in Japan in 2013 by KADOKAWA CORPORATION, Tokyo.
English translation rights arranged with KADOKAWA CORPORATION,
Tokyo, through Tuttle-Mori Agency, Inc., Tokyo.

English translation © 2018 by Yen Press, LLC

Yen On
1290 Avenue of the Americas
New York, NY 10104

Visit us at yenpress.com
facebook.com/yenpress
twitter.com/yenpress
yenpress.tumblr.com
instagram.com/yenpress

First Yen On Edition: April 2018

Yen On is an imprint of Yen Press, LLC.
The Yen On name and logo are trademarks of Yen Press, LLC.

The publisher is not responsible for websites (or their
content) that are not owned by the publisher.

Library of Congress Cataloging-in-Publication Data
Names: Wagahara, Satoshi. | 029 (Light novel illustrator)
illustrator. | Gifford, Kevin, translator.
Title: The devil is a part-timer! / Satoshi Wagahara ;
illustration by 029 (oniku) ; translation by Kevin
Gifford.
Other titles: Hataraku Maousama!. English
Description: First Yen On edition. | New York, NY :
Yen On, 2015–
Identifiers: LCCN 2015028390 |
ISBN 9780316383127 (v. 1 : pbk.) |
ISBN 9780316385015 (v. 2 : pbk.) |
ISBN 9780316385022 (v. 3 : pbk.) |
ISBN 9780316385039 (v. 4 : pbk.) |
ISBN 9780316385046 (v. 5 : pbk.) |
ISBN 9780316385060 (v. 6 : pbk.) |
ISBN 9780316469364 (v. 7 : pbk.) |
ISBN 9780316473910 (v. 8 : pbk.) |
ISBN 9780316474184 (v. 9 : pbk.) |
ISBN 9780316474207 (v. 10 : pbk.)
Subjects: | CYAC: Fantasy.
Classification: LCC PZ7.1.W34 Ha 2015 | DDC
[Fic]—dc23
LC record available at
http://lccn.loc.gov/2015028390

ISBNs: 978-0-316-47420-7 (paperback)
978-0-316-47422-1 (ebook)

1 3 5 7 9 10 8 6 4 2

LSC-C

Printed in the United States of America

PROLOGUE

The clock's hands were already showing two in the morning. It was a time that any respectable student would likely spend asleep, but Chiho Sasaki had marched straight from Ueno-Onshi Park to Room 202 of the Villa Rosa Sasazuka apartment building undeterred. Suzuno Kamazuki, the room's usual tenant, was gone.

"What's up? This ain't exactly my place, but c'mon in."

Tossing the schoolbag she had filled with her things toward a corner, she took a moment to look around the apartment. It felt like it'd been a while since her last visit, and current events were all just too weird to think about—that the tenant here was out traveling with the man she loved. Not in Japan, not even on Earth. All so they could find—and rescue—two other people Chiho held dearly.

Watching over Room 202 was Amane Ohguro, her outfit exposing ample amounts of her tanned skin and her long, black hair casually tied back. She was Chiho's former boss, more or less—they had signed a contract along those lines and everything, back when she helped out at the Ohguro-ya beachside snack bar in Choshi for a bit. But there was one important difference between Amane and Mayumi Kisaki, manager at the MgRonald location that Chiho normally worked at:

She wasn't exactly…normal.

If Amane was to be believed, she had regular physicals and always received a clean bill of health from them. Biologically, she was *Homo sapiens*, pretty much. But…

"Eesh, today was a hot one, wasn't it? You want some barley tea, maybe? Suzuno said it was okay to use whatever she's got in the fridge."

"Oh, okay. I'll go get some."

Instead of sitting down, Chiho headed to the large, state-of-the-art refrigerator, grabbing a bottle of tea, a couple of glasses from underneath the sink, and an ice tray from the pull-out freezer drawer. Before long, two glasses of iced tea were on a tray in the low table in the center of the room.

"Ooh, all prim and proper, eh?" marveled Amane as she sized up Chiho's clear familiarity with Suzuno's kitchen.

"Yeah," Chiho listlessly replied as she sat across from her, "I've been using her kitchen for a while now, so..."

"Here? What for?"

Chiho replied with a simple smile, sizing up Amane's expression.

"Mm? What is it?" Amane asked.

"Sorry. I was just thinking that, y'know, I was cooking here more often before we all went to Choshi. Just before we started working for you."

"Yeah?"

It had begun with Alas Ramus (the supposed "daughter" of the Hero and the Devil King) appearing at Villa Rosa Sasazuka, and had ended with the archangel Gabriel traveling to Japan to take the girl away. Alas's "parents" had stepped up to prevent that abduction, but subsequently, the wall of Room 201 had sported a gigantic hole that made it a bit difficult to inhabit the space effectively. Following that series of events, Alas Ramus fused with Emi's holy sword, thus saving her hide, but thanks to that, Emi was forced to visit Villa Rosa even more frequently so that Alas Ramus could see Maou.

Ashiya, who usually handled all domestic responsibilities in Devil's Castle (aka Room 201), then began regularly borrowing the kitchen in Room 202 to do the cooking, the hole in their own space proving too enormous to work around. And with Chiho never failing to supply them with extra provisions during this ordeal, she naturally wound up in Suzuno's kitchen a fair bit of the time. It wasn't anything that anyone strove for, but somewhere along the line the entire group found itself regularly sitting around the same dinner table, and nobody even thought to question it.

After that, when the landlord asked them to vacate the premises so she could fix the hole, it was Amane and the Ohguro-ya shop she ran who saved the day. And, looking back, it seemed like between Maou and Emi, the seven of them had started to do quite a few things together beyond their regular meals.

The Ohguro-ya gig didn't last long, but by the time the repairs were done and everyone was back in Sasazuka, regularly sharing the evening meal together was just the new normal. The Devil King and the Hero, archenemies; one an alien from another planet, the other an alien from another plane of existence. Just a scant year or so ago, none of them would have dreamed of eating in the same room, but now...well, it wasn't exactly all smiles, but they were bickering, carrying on, and (most importantly) *spending time* with one another.

Now that impossible kind of "peace" was disturbed. Now, around this building, there was no one left but Chiho, Amane, and Hanzou Urushihara, Room 201's sole remaining resident.

"You know, though, Amane..."

"Hmm?"

"How much do you really know about Maou and everyone, anyway?"

"Oh..." Amane looked up at the ceiling, finger on her chin. "Well, not that much. Just, like, Maou's not really from Earth, or all that human, either. Something corrupted...or, well, judging by the dark force he's got, I assume he's a demon or monster or something. And based on what Ashiya and Yusa and that black chicken told me, he used to have a whole wagonload of power, but something... Like, people like Yusa wielded this more purified type of power against him and forced him to flee into this world. And the power streaming around this world is all set up so it's neither 'positive' nor 'negative,' so he can't get any more demonic force from it, so he got a Joe-Shmoe job so he can feed himself. That's about what I can surmise, anyway."

"...That's... That's a lot to surmise..."

This was almost everything anyone needed to know about Maou's origins, in a neat little package.

"But who'd you hear all that from? The landlord? I've never met her, but…"

"Oh, Aunt Mikitty? You haven't, Chiho?"

"I saw her belly dancing in a video once."

"Huh?"

"Uhhm…"

"I didn't really 'hear' it from anyone. Just surmised it based on what I've seen, is all. Was I right?"

"Um, yeah, there's pretty much nothing to add to that…"

"Ah-ha-ha! You look disappointed." Amane let out a small sigh at Chiho's mixed signals. "But, you know, even I was able to come up with that much. Someone like Aunt Mikitty or my dad, they'd probably guess his age and blood type, too."

"I, uh, I don't get how they could do that, but… So then, um…"

"Hmm? Oh, right. You wanted to ask me about something else, didn't you?"

Chiho, the wind fully absent from her sails, still leaned her body forward. Amane reacted by flashing a world-beating smile and taking a hefty swig of barley tea. Then she winced.

"…Ooh, I think I got brain freeze…arg…"

"Um…" Chiho stared at her blankly.

"Ah-ha-ha-ha! Sorry, sorry… But, you know. People are weird that way. I can whip a horde of slavering demons with one hand tied behind my back, but whenever I belt down something too cold, boom! Instant headache, right around my temples. Although…"

Suddenly, Amane stood up, leaving her glass on the low table. She closed the window they had open for ventilation and leaned a hand against the wall separating them from Room 201.

"Amane?"

"Well, I'll tell you, Chiho, like I said I would. Just to you, though… Hmm…"

Chiho could spot Amane applying a bit more pressure with her index finger to the wall. She couldn't tell what was happening on the other side, but the vibration that ran across the floor—like something had just been slammed against it repeatedly—told her what she needed to know.

"Just in case, I'll take some measures to make sure nobody can eavesdrop on us. This is a pretty old apartment, and we wouldn't want Urushihara picking up on anything, would we?"

"...I guess not," Chiho said, face stiffened as she nodded. She hadn't gone out and said it, but the reason she suggested that Urushihara hole up in his apartment (and its wafer-thin walls) once he got back was precisely so that he could hear whatever Amane told her. She figured he'd get the hint—he had an instinct for that kind of thing, somehow—but the thoughtless gesture had been rewarded with what sounded like some rather painful "measures." Her eyes indicated to Chiho that, while she was willing to keep her promise to the letter of the word, she knew full well what the girl was scheming.

"...So let me ask you again," Chiho began, not commenting on it. She'd have to apologize to Urushihara later, but if Amane wasn't being too forthcoming, she had to stay on the offensive if she wanted anything at all out of her.

"Wow, you're gonna take notes? You're that serious?"

Chiho gave her a heavy nod, hands full with the three-color pen and notebook she'd taken from her bag, tools she normally used at work. "I always write things down when I hear them for the first time," she explained. "I got in the habit back when I had to memorize a bunch of stuff for work, like...right when I started sharing shifts with Maou."

Whenever you're plunged into a world you don't understand, the first order of business is to comprehend—to learn. That was something that someone important to Chiho had taught her long ago.

"Yeah?" Amane said as she sat back down and locked gazes with Chiho. "Well, whaddaya wanna know?"

Chiho took a deep breath. She tried to put everything together in her mind—what she'd seen, what had happened, what she needed to talk about—and the first question she had to ask suddenly seemed obvious.

"If the Earth has a Sephirot Tree of Life and Sephirah jewels coming from it, where is it right now? What kind of situation is it in?"

"Er..." Amane had seemed perfectly calm and composed before. But now, with Chiho's question, she looked caught off guard.

"Um, Chiho?"

"Yes?"

"Ah...I'm sorry, but that's just...a little beyond what I was expecting. I mean... Like, what kind of thought process led you to that question? 'Cause...you know, I was kind of expecting you to ask about who me or Aunt Mikitty really are, or what demon power is, or what happened on the beach in Choshi, or... I don't know. Something else!"

"Well, of course I'm wondering about that, too," Chiho quietly replied. "I just figured if I could get to the core of this first, we'd probably visit all those other things, too, so..."

"Aw, man... Really?"

"Maybe I shouldn't put it this way, but...if I had to guess, Amane, you're probably not that major a part of it all."

"No, but... I'm sorry; I probably shouldn't act all shocked like this. I'll tell you, okay? I'm just impressed you made it that far all by yourself, is all. Did you talk to Maou or someone along those lines?"

"No, not really in particular...but I wasn't alone in it, either." Chiho steadied her grip on her pen and notebook. "I mean, all this time I've spent with Maou and Yusa, I've been exposed to all these things, little by little. I try not to let any snippets of information escape me; I try to remember it all... So these aren't questions I came up with entirely by myself. It was Maou, it was Yusa, it was Urushihara, Suzuno, Alas Ramus, Erone... You too, of course, and Camio and the Malebranche guys, and Sariel and Gabriel, and...um..."

Chiho pointed at her own right hand.

"The memories of the woman who gave me this ring."

"So that purple one's the ninth?" Amane looked at the ring on Chiho's finger, the one with said purple jewel on it. Her face soured. "Boy, it looks like it's been put through the wringer. The lady who gave that to you's from Ente Isla or whatever, right?"

"She didn't explicitly say that, but I'm sure she is. I couldn't really tell you if she's human, though…"

"Ahh, same difference. As long as you can talk to them all right."

"In any event, if I want to take everything I've heard and everything I've experienced and wrap it all into one question, that's pretty much the one."

"All right. I gotcha. Not to be too persistent, but can I do something before I tell you?"

"Sure, but…? Agh!"

Without waiting for a reply, Amane placed a hand upon Chiho's forehead. Whatever she was searching for, she didn't find it. She shrugged and nodded.

"Hmm… No, I guess you're not connected to anything."

"Wh-what was that?"

"Sorry. I was just thinking the lady who gave you that was still secretly connected with you, but I guess she didn't go that far, huh? You said she put some memories into you, so if she's still peeking at your mind, then I just wasted my time teaching Urushihara a lesson."

This proved, at the very least, that Urushihara had been taught "a lesson" for spying. Chiho swore to herself that she'd apologize for getting him involved.

"Right. So you wanna know about Earth's life-tree and the Sephirahs…"

"So there is one? And with multiple Sephirahs?"

"Man, mind like a steel trap, huh? You don't have to keep double-checking everything. I'm not gonna lie to you."

"S-sorry." Chiho took a breath, regretting the way she was leaning so heavily over the table, and tried to lend an earnest ear to Amane. Not that it fazed her, though—if she didn't understand something, she intended to keep asking questions until she did. Maou had taught her that, too: If two repetitions aren't enough, go for three. That was how valuable, how meaningful, Amane's revelations would be.

"I'll start with the Sephirahs. Right now, they aren't in the same place as Earth's life-tree. They were scattered all over ages ago. And by 'ages,' I'm talking about the kinda times you're probably learning about in history class."

"So kind of recently, then?"

"Hmm?"

"Well, I mean, if it'd be covered by history class, they got separated somewhere in a timeline I'd still be able to comprehend, right? 'Cause I was picturing, like, millions of years before there was life on Earth."

"...You high schoolers can sure scale up time in your minds pretty fast these days, huh? If you actually lived that whole time, I'm sure you'd think it was a pretty darn long while, but...anyway. So if you don't mind me cutting to the chase, I wasn't born directly from a Sephirah the way Alas Ramus and Acieth were from theirs. You can kinda picture me as having one human parent, and one born from a Sephirah like those two. Sort of. I mean, even putting it that way is pretty weird, but—"

"Um, hang on a second."

That sequence alone held a treasure trove of information. First, both Alas Ramus and Acieth were blessed with impossibly long lifespans. Second, they could have human partners and create offspring with them. Third, they could pass their powers as Sephirah children down to the next generation. That much was clear simply by Amane's powers.

"So," Amane continued once Chiho was done jotting all this down, "it was my father who was born from a Sephirah. I guess his real name is Mumleed, born from the Sephirah Binah, but he goes by Tenji Ohguro these days."

"Mumleed... Does that mean anything special?"

Suzuno had mentioned that both "Alas Ramus" and "Acieth Alla" meant things in an Ente Isla language. "Erone" had to be something, too, although Chiho hadn't found out what yet. The same rule had to apply to Earth's Sephirah.

"Um... What was it? I think it meant, like, the 'mother ship' or something similar. Even though he's a guy and all."

Amane grinned.

"So to get back to your first question, Chiho—where the Earth's life-tree was."

"Y-yeah?"

Chiho swallowed nervously. These trees, and the Sephirah they bore, lay at the very core of the events surrounding her, Maou, and Emi. Between what Amane just said and what that woman implanted into her mind hinted at, there was no doubting the fact that Earth had its own tree of life. If she wanted to learn about Ente Isla's tree, she had to know everything she could about Earth's. And now that piece of info was dangling in front of her. The thought of being so close to the truth excited Chiho—enough that she didn't quite notice the verb tense Amane chose to use.

"It's somewhere," she began, "you can always see, but I'm afraid you wouldn't be able to reach it, Chiho."

"Somewhere I can always see?"

"Yeah, pretty much every day. Not so much when it's raining, though. Up there."

Amane raised her arm and pointed a finger toward the window. Chiho followed it, then gasped. There was the moon, shining brightly in the night sky.

"On...the Moon?"

The "tree of life" assigned to Earth was the Moon, its sole satellite.

As that fact took hold, a storm began to flash through Chiho's mind. And then, the moment all the information strewn about by this storm neatly organized itself in her mind, Chiho shuddered.

"Sariel's powers are stronger...the closer he is to the Moon... The most valuable thing in heaven... So heaven and the demon realm on Ente Isla is..."

"What? Was it that surprising to you?"

"N-n-no, I mean, yes, but, um, can you just keep going?"

Chiho's shaky hand sent her pen racing across the page as she tried to keep her thoughts from fluttering into thin air.

"Oh? Well, you probably figured out since I call her my aunt all the time, but Aunt Mikitty's the older sister of my father, which means Miki Shiba's another Sephirah child. She's a little different from the other Sephirahs, though, given her role in everything..."

Chiho nodded as she kept on writing. She had no idea if any of this connected to her future, but all this material that helped her ponder that future was raining down upon her like precious jewels pouring out from a treasure chest of secrets. She felt oddly exhilarated as she scribbled away, bringing a light smile to her face.

Suddenly:

"Aghh!!!!"

Amane's voice was stopped by a scream. Chiho's eyes darted around. The voice belonged to Urushihara. It sounded deeply pained—but if anything, Amane sounded worse.

"Wait... What? Why?! Why can he hear me? I put up a full guard and everything..."

Chiho didn't much appreciate how Amane was more concerned about Urushihara snooping on them than what had just happened to him. But either way, this was an emergency. Now, of all times, didn't seem right at all for a demon or angel to try attacking them, and Chiho was pretty sure Amane could handle either possibility with ease. But she stood up anyway, instinctively trying to figure out how to handle this.

Then...

""...!"""

There was a knock on the front door.

It was soft, but to Chiho's ears, it sounded refined, elegant, like a brass door knocker rapped against the massive doors of a stately mansion.

THE DEVIL LOSES HIS SOCIAL STANDING

The types of meticulously crafted multicourse meals Emi was being presented with suggested nothing of camping on a battlefield.

And yet they did nothing to stimulate her appetite. She knew she had to eat to keep up her physical strength, to say nothing of her mental outlook, but there was nothing in her that could make it happen.

It was silly to think about, but until she had been captured by Olba and made into the so-called Supreme Commander of the Phaigan Volunteer Force, Emi had no idea that food on Ente Isla could be so exquisite, so profoundly flavorful. And it wasn't because she had never eaten it before—she just had been unaware it even existed.

Being raised in a Western Island farming village meant that she'd enjoyed a warm family life, but not a well-funded one. And she'd certainly never left the area before the Devil King's Army had come onto the scene.

And yet, even during her hero's journey, they had to keep a careful eye on their funds, no matter how high-born Emeralda and Olba were. Even the resistance army's commanders couldn't count on being treated by princes and nobles, and they had been unlikely to see even what a commoner would consider a feast more than once a month or so.

In terms of variety in her diet, at least, the two years and change Emi had spent on Earth had far outclassed the sixteen she'd spent on Ente Isla. Now, though, the three meals presented to her and Alas Ramus on a daily basis used nothing but first-class ingredients prepared by first-class chefs. Comparing it to her usual war rations, or even to what she enjoyed in Japan, was ridiculous.

But it still wasn't right.

"Mommy, this isn't Suzu-Sis's corn soup!"

One mouthful was all it took for Alas Ramus to grimace.

"No? Well, how about this fried rice?"

It couldn't have been much different from the kind of fried rice they had in Japan, but she still took up a spoonful of the vaguely rice-like grain whipped up with a few other mystery ingredients and presented it to the child. She took a mouthful, and that was the end of it.

"This isn't like Al-cell's!"

"Well, I'm sorry, but this is all we have. Could you just make do with that, please?"

Even the most extravagant of the cuisine on offer in Efzahan couldn't compete with the comfort food made in the dingy, ill-stocked kitchen of a Tokyo apartment slum.

"What do you think of this fried chicken? You like fried chicken, right? I'll cut it up for you, so—"

"I like Chi-Sis's!"

As a mom, it would normally be Emi's job to chide Alas Ramus for being such a picky eater. But Emi couldn't drum up the willpower. She didn't need Alas Ramus to spell it out for her—she felt the exact same way. No matter how masterful the dish, having it served on the coldest, most unwelcome of dining tables would dull anyone's taste buds.

"You're going to be hungry later tonight if you don't eat anything. It doesn't taste bad, does it? Come on, let's have some."

"Awwww…"

Alas Ramus stared at her plate, pouting. That part of her, at least, was toddler-like to the extreme. She'd have these moments when, if something didn't pass muster with her, she'd fight it tooth and nail. That happened to be her meals right now, and Emi couldn't let her simply choose not to eat for the rest of her childhood. So she cajoled the child with a tactic she immediately regretted.

"Look, Alas Ramus. Once we're back home, we can have Bell and Alciel cook for us again, all right? So for just—"

"When can we go home?"

"..."

They couldn't.

Not even in her dreams.

The steaming dishes on the table began to cloud up in her eyes.

"There's nothing enticing about food you didn't do anything to earn, is there...?"

She did everything she could to compose herself and rein the tears back, face turned away from Alas Ramus.

"But...we have to eat...all right?"

Emi soothed her child, and then the tasteless meal continued.

✳

Emi's old wheat fields—the only proof that her father had ever existed—were being held hostage, forcing her to engage in a military campaign in which she had no interest. It was the work of Olba and Raguel, both pursuing her "warpower" in naming her supreme commander of a volunteer force created to rid Efzahan of demons.

To an entire people, she was a flag of hope, a rallying cry as the armies marched for the imperial capital of Heavensky to free it from the Malebranche that lurked its streets. But as far as Emi knew, it was Olba himself who had dragged the Malebranche into Efzahan. His actions were still totally opaque to her.

Meanwhile Ashiya, taken to Ente Isla by Gabriel, was once again made to descend upon Heavensky as Alciel, the Great Demon General. He had to, because otherwise he would be in danger, and the Malebranche tricked by the heavenly world to invade Efzahan would be in danger—even Maou, over in Japan, wasn't safe.

And as the table began to be set for a decisive confrontation between Emi's ·volunteer force and Ashiya's Malebranche hordes, Maou, Suzuno, and Acieth Alla—a being similar in origin to Alas Ramus—were traveling in Ente Isla to "rescue" the three of them. They had entered the world a distance away from the powder keg of the capital to avoid heavenly attention, but now they were proceeding as fast as their scooters could take them across the Eastern Island, gathering intel and approaching Heavensky.

Along the way, Suzuno had been disturbed to discover that the mood among island residents wasn't all that terribly gloomy, despite being ruled over by demons. It beat the Devil King's Army in their eyes, at least. The revelation had driven her to confront Maou, and the results had taught her something new about the demon realms.

Thanks to Albert, a former companion of Emi's they had the good luck to bump into, they had a bead on Emi's location, the volunteer force gathering around the capital, and what had to be done to settle all of this. They concluded that the sheer strength Maou could wield as Devil King, fused with Acieth and wielding a holy sword of his own, was essential—the key to the whole plan.

Or it should have been. But for some reason, Maou couldn't summon Acieth's sword. Not only did their fusion produce neither demonic nor holy force—the latter the type that Chiho had unleashed to save her school—it made him vomit up something that never should have been vomited up in the first place.

The force ensconced within these two holy pairings—Emi's holy force with Alas Ramus's sword; Maou's dark force with Acieth Alla's blade—was overwhelming. But now it was gone, and there was no other way to end this battle quickly. Maou was starting to worry that the week he had taken off from his job at MgRonald wouldn't be enough, and the thought made him tremble with fear.

✳

On the outer edge of the region referred to as the capital of Heavensky, there was a village, a sort of satellite city. There, in a dimly lit inn chamber, Sadao Maou was gritting his teeth and glaring at the two people looking down upon him.

"...I want an apology," he grumbled.

"Where did that come from, out of the blue?"

"Enough. Just apologize to me."

"Care to explain what on earth you are talking about first?"

"Do you two seriously think you can treat me like this and get away with it?"

"Hmph!" Suzuno Kamazuki, dressed in her Church garments instead of her usual Japanese kimono, rolled her eyes. "A fine thing to say. We are merely taking consideration for your safety."

Albert Ende, the mountain sage whose bulging muscles made Suzuno look like his daughter when they stood next to each other, nodded. "Y'know she's right, Devil King."

"How is this for my safety? I've never been so humiliated in my life."

"Well, whaddaya want from us?" Albert countered long-sufferingly, scratching his head. "All you've been doing the past two days is eat and sleep, Devil King."

"You've got some nerve, Albert, treating me like Urushihara or something... You can't just go around saying that..."

"U-ru-shi-ha-ra?" Albert turned to Suzuno for guidance. She just shrugged and shook her head.

"So be it," she lamented. "In a mere day's time, we will reach Heavensky Keep, the very heart of the capital. We are about to strike at our enemy's stoutest of strongholds. And yet look at you."

She turned her eyes away from Maou. There she saw Acieth Alla, sleeping atop a humble but clean-looking bed, a breadcrumb from the sweet-vinegar fried freshwater fish she had for lunch still stuck to the side of her content-looking lips.

"Devil King, you are completely useless to us in battle like this, all right? But if something happens to you, Chiho and Alas Ramus would be crushed. Our only choice is to sequester you at this inn for the time being."

"...Damn it!"

Maou gritted his teeth, faced with the painful truth, and punched the wall as hard as he could.

"Arrghh!!"

The pain from his first made him gurgle in anguish.

"Look, Devil King, stayin' here's for your own good, okay? That punch would've razed a city block in your heyday, but you didn't even dent the plaster. You go out in battle, and the Inlain Crimson Scarves would have you for lunch, to say nothin' of Olba."

"Rrrnnghh..."

Albert wasn't nearly a match to Emi when it came to antagonizing Maou, but he was still his current archnemesis, technically speaking. And yet here the man was, lecturing Maou with these eyes full of compassionate pity. Nothing could humiliate a Devil King more.

"Yo! Acieth!"

"Mngh?"

No longer able to stand the truth—that he was a Devil King in name only—Maou woke up the blissful-looking Acieth, grabbing one of the shoulder straps on her overalls and shaking it violently.

"What the hell's the problem, man?! Why isn't my demonic force coming back?! And what happened to that power you had back at Chi's school, huh?! Do you not understand what moderation is?!"

"......"

Acieth was too busy trying to refocus her eyes at first after Maou's violent outburst to answer. But after he stopped shouting, the answer came softly.

"...Shrimp..."

"Shrimp?! What about shrimp?!"

"If I eat grilled shrimp, maybe I know?"

"..."

Maou silently raised a fist, eyes wild. Suzuno had to expend a surprising amount of strength to stop him.

"H-halt, Devil King! This is accomplishing nothing! I understand how you feel, but you must not!"

"Lay off, Suzuno. This is an era of equal rights. I can hit anybody I want!"

"Equal rights or not, you have a duty to uphold your pride, you monster!"

"See, this is exactly why people keep belittling the Men's Rights movement—"

"You're doing a fine job belittling yourself!!"

The pointless bickering continued for a few moments more, but in terms of physical strength, Maou was no longer a match for Suzuno. He dolefully took his hands off of Acieth.

"Tch. No shrimp, huh…?"

With perhaps the one rejoinder that would rankle Maou the most right now, Acieth went back to her dreams. This time, Albert had to help keep Maou away, too.

"Owwww! All right! I get it!"

Suzuno had more than enough strength in a pinch, but Albert's body was on a whole other dimension. Pinned down by these two tanks, the Devil King and former international tyrant teared up as he worked through his desire to kill Acieth.

"Geez, cut me some slack, guys…owww…"

Now his whine came at a lower volume as he rubbed his almost-dislocated shoulders. He knew what kind of look Suzuno and Albert were giving him.

"I mean, come on! What the hell…?" he asked, whining as he balled up and unclenched his fists.

His demonic power wasn't coming back. It was a shock to realize, and it was completely beyond Suzuno's reckoning. If they wanted to bring Emi and Ashiya home to Japan together, it'd be impossible to avoid combat with archangels. They knew Gabriel and Camael were nearby and aching for a fight. And while Suzuno knew the powers of her war hammer, she also knew she was nothing compared to Emi fused with Alas Ramus. Even taking on Albert in a one-on-one match would probably end with her eating dirt—and Albert would never win against Emi at full strength.

Trying to challenge two archangels without Maou's power to count on produced no hope of victory. Perhaps they could make contact with Emi and have her wield her angel-busting powers to punch them all an easy ticket off the planet. But that wouldn't be enough. If that was all it took to wrap this up, Emi would've done so long ago. This whole uproar was about more than taking Emi and Ashiya back to Japan. They had to push the reset button on whatever situation both of them were in right now, and they had to do so in a way that ensured nobody launched an attack on Japan. And it was more than just beating up the villains who took their friends—they had to "clean things up" after the battle, ensuring that nobody had any political or military motivations for Emi or Ashiya any longer.

The scenario Suzuno pictured at one point placed enormous importance on Maou using his holy sword to handle both the battle and the cleanup afterward. Now summoning so much as a dollar-store kitchen knife was apparently enough to make Maou's intestines churn. She would have to go with Plan B, and that would have to involve Albert, their quest's unexpected windfall.

"Cheer up, Devil King," the burly man attempted. "It's not your fault. And it's not the kinda thing cursing at yourself's gonna solve."

"Yeahh, but if this is how it's gonna be, why the hell did I take all those extra shifts to get time off for this thing?! I'm just sitting here! Eat, sleep, wander around like some tourist!"

To Maou, the fate of every inch of land that spread across the Eastern Island of Ente Isla was equal on the scales with the fate of his future shift schedule.

Suzuno, for different reasons, shook her head. "This was something we could never have foreseen," she said. "Besides, if you had not made that transformation before, neither I, nor Chiho, nor Lucifer would have survived. This state of affairs, too, must mean something for us. So stop sulking. If you call yourself king, look at the whole picture, not only what lies in front of you."

"Yeah, but…"

"I am not interested in seeing you leap into battle without access to your skills, only to pay dearly for it. Just wait for us to return. I promise you that before long, Emilia, her father, Alas Ramus, and Alciel will be back with us."

"Suzuno…"

As if to stop him before he began, Suzuno knelt down in front of Maou, still seated on his bed, and locked eyes with him as she took his hand.

"I, and Emilia, have gone on and on about how you are our enemy, only to latch on to your powers every time at the end of it. This time, at least, I hope you will let us repay the favor. That, as your general in the New Devil King's Army, is my advice to you."

"I love how you never bring that up except when it helps you, man."

"Indeed. I have come to learn that you have a weakness against it." Suzuno let out a wry smile as she stood up and patted the dust off her vestments. "Besides, is it not the job of a commander to lie back in a safe haven and watch what his troops are doing?"

"That's really not my style."

"If something sinister comes your way, avoid it. Run away. That is how people live their lives."

"Hey," Albert interjected, unnerved by how oddly friendly Suzuno and Maou were, "I don't know what you folks were up to on Earth, but I've got no intention of siding with the Devil King. Just so we're clear on that?"

He had approved of Emi staying in Japan for the time being, but the idea of his working together with Satan, King of All Demons, was stretching his moral compass to unhealthy lengths.

"I know," Suzuno replied. "But just this once, we need as many companions on our side as we can gather."

"Companions, eh?" Albert shrugged, his eyes indicating he didn't find the concept entirely revolting. "If that's how you put it, then this is a hell of a lot more complex than I thought."

"There's something I've been wanting to ask, though," Maou added.

"Yes?"

"Why are you and Emeralda so keen on letting Emi stay in Japan without killing me? Like, I know you want her to have her freedom, but that only goes so far with you guys, right? 'Cause after Olba and Lucifer attacked, I was more worried about you and Emeralda than Emi—like, maybe you'd kill me without telling her or something."

"Ah, we did deliberate over that."

"Oh, geez, you did?"

Albert seemed to relish how comically Maou winced at the idea of an active cabal conspiring against him.

"I can't tell ya what Eme was thinking, but I had my own reasons not to try it. I wanted to respect Emilia's wishes, of course, but beyond that…"

He walked up to Maou and gave him a series of powerful, bear-like pats on the shoulder.

"Ow! What's that for?"

"I s'pose you've got that girl Sasaki and Adramelech to thank, huh?"

"Chi and…Adramelech?" Maou turned an eyebrow up at the unexpected mention of Chiho, as well as one of his now-deceased Great Demon Generals. Albert, however, merely shook his head.

"Right," said, "if we're going, we'd better get started soon. I s'pose I'll be leading the team, but the Phaigan Volunteer Force is just a day or two away from central Heavensky, too. If Emilia's really with them, then we'll have to blend in with all the chaos they'll drum up on the way to Heavensky Keep. In terms of distance, it's gonna be a pretty close shave. That's why you gotta stay here with that holy-sword lady, all right, Devil King?"

And with that, Albert paused just long enough to give the stunned Maou a side glance before walking out of the room.

Calling Heavensky a "city" was, in a way, not giving it enough credit. It was vast, expansive, and the nobles' quarter in the middle of it was packed with military buildings. This included the head-quarters for four of the upper armies composing the Eight Scarves of Efzahan—Inlain Azure, Regal Azure, Inlain Jade, and Regal Jade. They stood alongside the empire's main governmental offices, imperial courts, and embassies run by the foreign tribes that swore allegiance to the Azure Emperor. It had a lot of people to house, and it was therefore massive. If an army marched from the keep at normal speed, it would take more than a day simply to leave the central district's boundaries.

This district was surrounded by the so-called merchants' quarter, home to businessmen, upper-class non-nobles, and the lower four of the Eight Scarves—Inlain Citral, Regal Citral, Inlain Crimson, and Regal Crimson. The rule of thumb was that an army on the march would require another day to make their way out of this district.

In order to enforce borders and prevent invasions, castle walls snaked their way across the entirety of the central and merchant districts, part of them forming long, straight boundaries that extended all the way out to the far regions of the agricultural/industrial quarter outside of town.

These walls—running generally along the northeast, northwest, southeast, and southwest directions—were world-famous structures, huge edifices built long before the Azure Emperor's reign. They had seen wide-scale erosion on the island's west side, where things were generally peaceful through the years, but toward the east, where rebellious tribes still made the emperor fret over the potential for civil war, the government gathered people from across the land for "public works projects" to reinforce the walls once every few years, forming just as vital a defense as they did in ancient times.

The agricultural and industrial areas beyond the city spread out even farther and wider than either the central or merchant zones. It was the breadbasket of the capital and Efzahan in general, as well as the island's main manufacturing hub. The village whose inn Suzuno and Albert wanted to dump Maou at was beyond even this district, part of the string of satellite cities and travel stops along the Imperial Road, the wide, well-kept highway that stretched from Heavensky to most of the Eastern Island's populated areas.

"Thinking about it," Maou said before his demotion, as he looked at a map of the region, "things like trains and cars are actually pretty amazing, aren't they? I mean, from here to Heavensky's central district, that's pretty much the distance between the Keio Hachioji and Shinjuku stations, right? That's, like, not even half a day. Under two hours, even. But nobody would even think of walking that distance."

Albert was bewildered to hear this, but outside of the occasional culture shock, the journey between where they found him in Honpha and now had gone without a hitch. He had found a wagon caravan for them to travel on without being suspected, letting them travel from Honpha to just outside Heavensky without expending a drop of their scooters' precious gas supply.

He had a few advantages in this. For one, unlike Maou and Suzuno, he enjoyed total freedom of movement. Suzuno knew he had been working for Emeralda, one of Saint Aile's top leaders, to gather intelligence on the ground level. This agreement was strictly personal on Albert's part; he made no oath of fealty to Saint Aile, and he was no citizen of theirs. He had no political or national restrictions placed upon him, he had enough strength to carry him past almost anyone who breathed on Ente Isla, and he was blessed with both extensive travel experience and ample funding to tap into when needed.

Plus, as he put it: "Outta the people who defeated the Devil King, I'm the least known of 'em all. Saves me a lot of unnecessary effort trying to gather intel, y'know?" Which made sense. Emilia's name preceded her everywhere she went. Emeralda Etuva was the court sorceress of the holy empire of Saint Aile, the most powerful country on the Western Island. Olba Meiyer was one of the six archbishops at the very peak of Church bureaucracy. Albert, meanwhile, was a woodcutter from the north, a mountain sage—titles that didn't divulge a lot of details about his true nature.

That was by design, however. Even after the Devil King's Army was defeated, he still revealed little about his past. And between that and his apparent disinterest in returning home to the Northern Island, there just wasn't much conventional wisdom about him among the populace, compared to his three more famous companions. This meant people treated him little differently from anyone else, and that ensured the information he gathered was, by and large, reliable.

"Sir Albert," Suzuno asked as she adjusted the harness on a pair of horses tied to the nearby stable to suit her better, "what did you mean when you spoke earlier?"

These were stout war horses, again procured for them by Albert, and while more wide than tall, the breed they belonged to was built for long distances, well-suited for caravans and cavalry corps. With Maou out of the picture, Suzuno and Albert would be proceeding by themselves, but Albert (as to be expected) didn't know anything about driving a scooter around. Suzuno, on the other hand, was more than capable on the saddle. There was no reason not to switch to that, especially if they wanted to stay inconspicuous, although it was adding insult to injury for Maou given his complete lack of horsemanship skills.

"Hmm?" Albert said, lifting his head. "What about?"

"You said I would have Chiho and Adramelech to thank later."

"Oh, that?" he replied as he checked the stirrups of his own mount. "Well, I dunno if a Westerner like you would like to hear it much, but I pretty well knew from early on that the Devil King's Army wasn't here to destroy all mankind or anything. I knew some of the demons were pretty reasonable to work with, in fact."

"You did?"

"I usedta be the commander of the Fifteenth Mountain Corps, remember."

"Commander of them?" Suzuno couldn't hide her surprise. "That's a corps of elite soldiers from the clans that dot the Northern Island, is it not?"

The Northern Island was mainly populated by countless pockets of tightly knit clans and villages, spread out across the mountains that lined most of the continent. There were no broad, encompassing kingdoms like with Saint Aile or Efzahan—instead, from the cold expanses of the north to the mountains and coastlines below, a gaggle of warlords jostled against each other for what plains and territories existed. Representatives from each one were sent to a larger parliament that presided over island-wide matters, forming a federation that, while loose in structure, had stood the test of time so far.

The Mountain Corps was the most powerful military organization on the island, formed from clan warriors specially selected for their magic or martial-arts skills. They were bound by parliament regulations to stand up together and resist anything that threatened the Northern Island as a whole, and whenever they were summoned as such, a commander would be chosen among the participating clans in round-robin fashion. Albert was thus the commander of the Corps during the event of its fifteenth summoning.

One major difference between the Corps and the militaries of more established nations elsewhere was that, in the case of conflict between clans, individual Corps members were free to fight against each other for the sake of their own affiliation.

The balance of power differed wildly from other islands, for a number of reasons. For example, each clan held sway over a fairly small population. The land was rugged, mountainous, and arable only in small pockets. And with the distances often put in place between clan territories, it was nearly impossible for one clan to simply invade and conquer another. Thus, instead of wasting time spilling blood at the drop of a hat, the culture up north developed a system of official "contests" to resolve its wars. If a squabble was beyond the abilities of the parliament to settle, a few members of the Mountain Corps would battle it out in a predefined space.

This arrangement meant that few, if any, warriors ever died in battle. There were massacres here and there across history, of course, but without exception, the perpetrators of such tragedies would be branded "dangerous" by neighboring clans, face attack from all direction, and get annihilated. That, luckily, had not happened recently. Even the more serious disputes between clans as of late were resolved either through parliamentary conferences or contests held in the Northern Island Federation capital of Phiyenci, in an arena colloquially known as the Goat Pasture.

The Northern Island's geopolitical situation had evolved in a completely different direction from the rest of Ente Isla. A dizzying array of clans were involved with it, each with very different cultures and customs, and leading a Mountain Corps composed of such a motley crew of ethnicities and values indicated to Suzuno that Albert's leadership talents had to equal or exceed the generals from any other land.

"Well," Albert replied, "considerin' how we were pretty well wiped out by Adramelech's forces, nobody calls 'em 'elite' too often any longer."

"Oh, nothing of it..."

"It's the truth, though. I led the Fifteenth Mountain Corps straight into the slaughter against 'em. The longest casualty list of any Corps that came before it. We heard what was going on in Isla Centurum, so we were prepared for the worst when it came to our clans. Then Adramelech took the surviving Corps warriors and clan leaders and gathered them up in the Goat Pasture. And you know what he said?"

Adramelech, the bull-headed, spear-toting Great Demon General who was easily two to three times Albert's size, said this: "Our mission is not to massacre you. I will guarantee the lives of all clan members, but only if you expel from the continent any warriors who may resist the Devil King's Army and accept our rule over your land."

His words came with a warning for any Mountain Corps members willing to fight it out to the end: "Warriors, the time may come when you once more raise sword and shield against us, as long as you live and breathe. But if you believe it is a warrior's lot to waste his life on an unwinnable conflict and expose the clan he swore to protect to mortal danger, then you are nothing more than slavering beasts, baring your fangs and salivating for blood. If you still wish to fight, I will not stop you. But my spear will. And it will take all you hold precious with it."

Many in the Corps responded by falling upon their own blades, awash in the humiliation of being a survivor from a losing army. With those who did not, Adramelech kept his promise.

The Mountain Corps was dissolved, and once the last of its still battle-worthy members were escorted off the continent by the demons, the Northern Island never saw needless conflict again.

The exiled Corps soldiers, Albert included, made their way to the other islands, hoping to regroup and challenge Adramelech again. What greeted them, however, were conquered lands ruled by the Devil King's Army. There was no safe haven for them in which to plot their rebellion. Efzahan to the east, Saint Aile to the west, and the kingdom of Haruun to the south were all under demon rule—and they were the last forces with any chance at defying them. But the Mountain Corps were just an informal clutch of fighters; they had no diplomatic skills, they were scattered to the four winds, they weren't allowed to join so much as the mercenary forces of any neighboring nation, and most of them never returned to the Northern Island. It wasn't until the Hero Emilia freed the four islands that they saw each other again—and by then, they numbered less than half of what they used to.

"I'm not gonna say life was wonderful with the Devil King's Army, but at the end of it, Adramelech stuck to his word. My clan's elder said it himself—Adramelech wouldn't hesitate to brutally murder anyone who rose up against him, but he never killed anyone on a simple whim."

"I had no idea…"

"And when me, Emilia, Eme, and Olba faced him later on, I told 'im I wanted to take him on solo. I wanted a rematch, y'know? And what do you think happened? That bastard Adramelech refused me. He said if I was willing to throw away the battle for the sake of some cheap pride, mankind would never deserve to be freed from the demons. Even at the very end, I couldn't defeat him by myself."

There was no regret or anger written on Albert's face. All that remained was his memories of the battle.

"That was no demon. Nor a fighter, either. He knew what it took to abandon your own emotions, to stand tall against others and do what needed to be done. I guess 'politician' is the best way I could describe him. I let my pride blind me in battle, but he never allowed that for himself. He was a better man than I'll ever be. Pretty funny way to describe a demon, huh?"

"I am not sure I find it funny at all these days." Suzuno pulled at the reins, leading her horse out of the stable. Her eyes were pointed back at their inn.

"I guess not," Albert added with a chuckle. The inn, of course, currently housed a Devil King who kept pouting at the way people viewed him as a human. "And if that's how Adramelech was, there's no way the Devil King he served was any kind of crazed monster, either. 'Course, if I was from the west or south where there were a lot more massacres, I'd probably view it a bit differently. But either way, when Emilia started suggestin' she was in no hurry to kill the Devil King in Japan despite how much she hated him, I thought, hey, let's give her a little time to sort things out 'n' see what he's doing. Figure out who those 'demons' really were."

Suzuno recalled that moment, back on Earth, when she learned that angels were essentially the same as human beings. That, and the back-to-back conversations she had outside of Honpha the day before they found Albert. Maou's confession—the confession of a leader, a man whose outlook on life was no different from any human king's.

She turned her face aside, wincing. "…!"

"Something up?" a quizzical Albert asked.

"N-no, nothing."

She shook her head, trying to fight off her sudden agitation.

Why did I do something like that?

No matter what her views on demons were, there was no way Ente Isla would ever forgive Satan or his Devil King's Army. Understanding what lurked inside Maou's heart would provide nothing in the way of benefit to her. But there she was anyway, close enough to Maou that she could feel his body heat, listening to his most heartfelt words and neatly placing them into hers. There was nothing at all unpleasant about the experience. If anything, it was heartwarming.

She knew she wanted to help him overcome his self-doubt over what had happened to himself and his army.

But why did she have to be so kind to him? Suzuno shook her head, the spine that had touched Maou's suddenly feeling hot to the touch.

"…What about you, Albert?"

"Huh?"

"What do you think of Adramelech, as a single conscious creature?"

"A single conscious what?"

"No, I mean…"

Such a question was about the most inappropriate thing one could ask an Ente Islan. But it was the only way Suzuno could faithfully put what she wanted to ask into words.

"What kind of…'person' do you think Adramelech was?"

Albert flashed a carefree smile—one that indicated he knew all about the conflict in Suzuno's mind. He, after all, had seen with his own eyes the gap between what the world thought of the Devil King's Army and what he remembered about Adramelech.

"You're a funny girl, you know that? I never even talked about stuff like this with Eme." Another grin. "Can you promise not to tell anyone about this? It'd put me in a bad spot if you did. As a fighter, and as a leader of soldiers and citizens, Adramelech's pretty much my ideal. If he was human and appeared on the Northern Island scene three hundred or so years earlier, I bet we'd have a kingdom as rich 'n' powerful as Efzahan or Saint Aile by now."

"…You do?" Suzuno nodded, letting off a light smile of her own to match Albert's.

"So what're we gonna do now, though? 'Cause the way you acted around the Devil King, it sounds like you got a plan in mind."

Dwelling on the past was over. Now they had to turn their eyes toward the battle looming ahead. Suzuno gave a light nod and turned back toward the inn.

"With Acieth's sword unavailable to us, a massive head-on strike to save Emilia and Alciel stands little chance of succeeding. Instead,

we will go undercover to capture another person, ensuring that
Emilia's force has no motivation to continue any further. If we can
keep them from clashing with the capital's armies, Emilia has no
reason to fight Alciel, and it will earn us time to concoct another
plan to secure them."

Extra time, she thought, also gave Maou a chance to find some
way to recover his own powers. Such a leisurely approach would
take much longer than Maou's scheduled week, but that was nothing
compared to the safety of both their friends and the Eastern Island
itself.

"Oh? So what comes first?"

"We show them," Suzuno replied, "that they did not call me the
'fanatical dark side of the Church' for nothing."

She lifted the mask covering the bottom half of her head, fully
hiding her face underneath her robes.

"We will reach Heavensky's central district before the volunteers
do. Our mission is twofold. First, within the next twelve hours, we
find out where Nord Justina and the Azure Emperor are. The fate
of Nord is no doubt the heaviest of the shackles placed upon Emilia
right now, and the presence of the emperor is what pushes her force
forward. Second, if we can, we take them away from the influence of
the angels and Malebranche. That alone should prevent any major
battle."

"Are you…?!" Not even Albert could hide his surprise at the idea.
"Are you saying we kidnap the Azure Emperor?! From Heavensky
while it's crawling with Malebranche demons? And in half a day? It
might be possible, yes, but we'll have no time to rest, I'll tell you that
much!"

"It is possible. For us."

Suzuno nodded, as if nothing at all was crazy about her proposal.

Lifting the hem of her robe, she nimbly hefted herself up on her
ride's saddle. Two horses stepped out from the dim stable into the
bright afternoon sunlight, led by the resolute-looking Suzuno.

"I have had quite enough of humans and demons fighting without any idea what they fight for. Before all-out war erupts between Emilia and Alciel, we must hand the emperor over to the volunteer force and prevent the armies from ever seeing each other."

✳

Watching through the window as Suzuno and Albert spurred their horses and galloped away, Maou gritted his teeth, as if ready to start gnawing at the window frame.

They were right—in his current state, he would be nothing but a drag on the two of them. Kicking him off the front lines was absolutely the correct thing to do.

Maou and Acieth wielded awesome amounts of non-holy, non-demonic power on Earth, but neither that nor Maou's original demonic force had returned to him on Ente Isla. Trying to summon it only made him sick to his stomach.

"Maybe I'm out of it this time," he murmured to himself, "but I can't just sit here staring into space forever."

He knew he couldn't afford to be a passive spectator. He had to figure out why all this was happening to him, for it raised serious questions about both this rescue effort and his own future. Who could say if those powers would spring back to life if something happened to him back in Japan later?

There wasn't much to work with, but Maou had a few theories on why both his dark force and the mystery power he used to defeat Camael and Libicocco were gone. One was his merging with Acieth—the one major difference between then and now. The other: his current location, nowhere near Japan or Earth. Maou could do nothing about either factor, but they still gave him food for thought.

"What in the world was that power, anyway?"

He pondered over the enigmatic force that had saved the day at Sasahata North High School, only to disappear without a trace. The anxiety and frustration were enough to make him slap a hand against the window frame again. The noise was enough to make Acieth, still sleeping like an angel in bed, mutter a few words.

"My...my sister... Look at that... Wagyu beef..."

"You know you're neeeever gonna get that on our budget, right?"

At this unwelcome interruption of his melancholy, Maou gathered a sigh, and then:

"Hey! Acieth! Get up!"

"Waahah?!"

He smacked Acieth's pillow a few times, forcing her up.

"I was...was...b-b-b-b-b-big surprised... What's...? What was that, Maou? I was just about to eat Iberian pastrami sandwich..."

"Have you ever even eaten that? I kinda doubt Nord had that kind of luxury to give you!"

Maou helped her up, ignoring the fact that Acieth's menu ever-so-subtly shifted just before awaking.

"C'mon! We gotta start training!"

"Whuh? Training... You gonna puke again?"

"That's not something a proper girl should be saying, you know! That's exactly what I want to avoid, so we gotta train to figure out what's causing it!"

Maou's conviction seemed firm, but in the two days before they arrived at the inn, he had dry-heaved so often that Acieth's exasperation was understandable.

"Well," she said, "okay, if you want. I am pretty tired, like you, Maou."

"Oh?"

Acieth got out of bed and stretched her arms high, a look of discontent on her face. "I feel not very good, too. I am so hungry, all the time. Your power is not holy, Maou, so maybe not so good a match? I wish you were more kinder to me!"

Considering Acieth had eaten, slept, and lazed out the most out of anyone on this journey, this was less than convincing to Maou. But considering all the changes in his own body, it wouldn't be odd to think something similar was happening to his companion.

"...All right," he said, regretting the rude awakening he'd given her. "I'm sorry. But I can't just follow their orders and sit here all day. How 'bout we eat, and I can ask you a few questions along the way?"

"Hmm? Where did Suzuno and Albert go?"

She hadn't noticed their absence until now.

"They left us here," Maou replied, "but if we don't do something, this battle's gonna go on forever. You wanna see Alas Ramus ASAP, don't you? So gimme a little strength and knowledge to work with. Because otherwise I can't guarantee our safety when we join in later. Plus, I'll be out of a job."

Maou had been granted exactly one week for his Ente Isla road trip—the amount of time he eked out through some consummate shift-juggling work. Going past that would constitute going AWOL from work and the almost-certain end of his job in Japan. To Maou, this was impossible to accept.

"What?! They left us here, hanging with the bear?! How mean!"

"...Midair. Hanging in midair. At any rate, let's go eat."

He grabbed her hand before she could complain any further and headed for a nearby tavern.

"So to start, I want you to explain everything from the beginning. Why did you and Alas Ramus merge with us in the first place? What was it for?"

"I dunno. Ooh, take that stew for me, Maou!"

"Ugh, look..."

All Maou wanted to do was get at the core of his troubles. To Acieth, that wasn't as important as her next meal ticket. He winced as she tucked into the bowl, bits of pumpkin-like vegetables sticking to the sides of her mouth. She frowned at him.

"... Maou," she whined, "if you think answer is easy to give, you are wrong."

"Huh?"

"I don't know, too! Why I can merge with Pop or Maou, why I have to merge, why I can do this and that when we merge... I don't know."

It was a rare bout of logical thinking that erupted from Acieth as she polished off the root-vegetable stew. Maou took the initiative and decided to ask her about a certain term she used by Sasahata North High's front gate.

"You said something about a 'latent force' before, though, didn't you?"

"Maou, when did you learn that, um, the word 'eating' is when you eat food?"

"Um?"

"When the baby thinks 'Let's eat,' it eats, yes?"

"Umm?" Maou turned to his side, unable to grasp her point, but still keenly noting the salad bowl and plate of dumplings she was about to help herself to.

"It is process. You do something; you decide inside of you to do again; you learn that this thing you do, it is called 'eating'; then you learn what 'eating' does for you. Takes very long time. I know I can merge with Pop and you. I know I probably have to, for to keep living. I know it is called 'latent force.' But what does do for me? I don't know. None of us do, I don't think."

"Who's us?" Maou asked, leaning forward. He could see the conversation soon veering in another important direction.

"My sister, she talk to you? About Malchut or Gevurah or something?"

"Oh… So the other Sephirah take the form of human beings, too, like you guys and Erone?"

"You know Erone? Surprising!"

It was not surprising enough to make Acieth stop stuffing dumplings into her mouth, so she continued:

"Malchut is smartest of us. Good friends with my sister, and taught me lot of things, too. That is how I learn about 'latent force.'"

"…So where is he now?"

That was another concern for Maou. Malchut was a name Alas Ramus had mentioned several times. If he and all the other Sephirah out there took human form like the three he had personally seen, they could be well near anywhere. Or was it only the scattered Yesod fragments that were scattered worldwide, with the intact Sephirah all somewhere else?

"...I don't know. The last time I talk to him, it was long time ago."

"Look, if you start choking after you stuff your cheeks up like a chipmunk, I'm not gonna feel sorry for you, all right?"

Acieth gave him a crestfallen look, even as she held two different sweet dumplings in her hands, taking bites in rotation. If she didn't know, there was no point in Maou pursuing the question further.

"You know, though..."

"Yuh?"

Maou reached across the table and started patting Acieth's head, like he frequently did to Alas Ramus.

"We're just one step away from Alas Ramus, more or less. Let's see this to the end, okay?"

"Oh, is that all?" a peeved-looking Acieth countered before cramming in the remains of both dumplings at once. "Well, I will help with 'training,' but I really am hungry, you see? I will eat ten more of dumplings! Or I won't be strong!"

"Oh... Wait, *ten*?!"

Maou took a slack-jawed look at his own plate. These dumplings were packed with meat, vegetables, and something resembling noodles made from potato, all cut up, simmered, and wrapped up in dough with some flavorful broth. They were pretty hefty—and delicious, Maou admitted—but one of them alone was like eating two bowls of rice. Acieth plowing through two at once was enough of a shock; along with the soup and salad, about one and a half was all he could handle. The sticker price certainly reflected their size, too.

"Well," he said dejectedly, thinking about the coins he had in the leather pouch in his jacket, "I suppose we have the funds, but..."

The tab he'd have to pay was one thing, but this was technically Suzuno's money. They would presumably have Emi and Nord safe at the end of this, so maybe they could ask them to cover their expenses. But Maou was already useless to the party at the moment. He couldn't bear the thought of acting like an employee partying downtown all night and invoicing his boss for it the day after.

If you want to eat, you have to work. He had a firm, unbending allegiance to that philosophy. As a Devil King, and as a man, he couldn't allow himself to breezily eat and drink whatever he wanted with someone else's cash.

"...It's gonna be tough going," Maou muttered from the pit of his stomach.

Acieth nodded in response, then turned to the tavernkeeper, who happened to be passing by.

"Hey! Sir! Ten more dumplings!!"

"He doesn't speak Japanese, dude." Without any Idea Link skills, Maou had to rely on his budding Yahwan abilities. "<Master, please give us ten more dumplings.>"

"<Did you say...ten?>" came the stunned reply.

"<You may not believe it, but this child will eat them. I think she likes them. We are not in a hurry, so if you could...>"

The tavernkeeper gave Acieth an astonished glance. She responded by meekly nodding, her smile running from ear to ear.

"<Well, sir, my son's a pretty big eater, too, but not even he could accomplish that feat. But you got it.>"

He wandered into the kitchen and came back five minutes later. Peeking past the door, Maou spotted a series of large stacked baskets, each one brimming with steam. They must have made a fair number of them in advance.

"<I'll wrap up whatever you don't eat.>"

And there they were: ten dumplings, each on their own little plate atop a larger tray, like little pillows for gnomes.

"What did he say, Maou?"

"Like, if you can't eat them all, they'll wrap them up for us."

"...Oh?"

Acieth gave a sly grin, as if the tavernkeeper had just challenged her to a duel.

"He will regret the saying of that!"

The next moment, she was a whirlwind of gluttony, tearing at the tray of "pillows" like a starved wolf.

"Erf. No more."

"You are *such* a disappointment!"

Acieth threw in the towel immediately after consuming dumpling number seven. She always tended to eat a lot, so he was expecting her to scarf them down like a participant in a hot-dog-eating contest. By the end of the fourth, however, she was clearly slowing down. It was still an astounding feat given her slight frame, but considering all her grandstanding beforehand, the results *were* a bit of a letdown.

The glasses of water Acieth kept ordering in between were another punch in the gut for Maou. Efzahan had ample water supplies nationwide, but unlike in Japan, they didn't just hand out glasses for free at restaurants. Counting the refills as they came was even more depressing than counting the dumplings. All with Suzuno's money, he constantly reminded himself.

"<…Excuse me,>" he droned as if in a daze, "<we will eat the rest at the inn, so could you wrap these up?>"

"<Oh, of course. She eats about as much as my son does, you know. Not too bad a showing!>"

Maou didn't appreciate the compliment. All that food she ate, and they were supposed to be engaging in physical activity after this. He had a feeling that, no matter what mysteries they tackled today—holy energy, dark energy, swords, Ente Isla, latent forces—it would probably end in puking.

The sense of foreboding that formed a dark cloud over Maou's head at first caused him not to notice the series of loud explosions from outside. He looked up, and so did Acieth, who made a yelp like a yeti from some snowy mountain.

"<Oh, that?>" the tavernkeeper said, noting their reactions. "<Just some firecrackers. They light them to fend off evil spirits. You know how it's been lately—the Azure Emperor declaring war on

everybody, demons filing back into Heavensky, Phaigan sending a volunteer force or whatever after them. Just when we thought things were stable again, all this stuff is putting the whole village on edge. Usually they light 'em at the start of the year as a peace offering, though.>"

"<...Oh.>"

Between what Gabriel and others had told him, Maou and his friends knew that the Phaigan Volunteer Force was on their way to Heavensky from the port city of Phaigan. They had already heard rumors that Emilia the Hero was among their ranks. But as that woman at the tavern in Honpha had said, to the average person in Efzahan it didn't really matter whether the Azure Emperor or the Malebranche demons were in control of the empire. A fatalistic view, but one that was endemic nationwide.

"<...Well,>" Maou asked, "<how would *you* like this country to turn out?>"

"<Oh, who knows? As long as I can put food on the table tomorrow, I'm not gonna be picky.>"

"<That's good enough for you?>"

"<What else can I ask for? That's the kind of country this is. The Eight Scarves are going on about how the tribes to the east could use this chaos to stage a coup, but who knows how true that is, either.>" He shrugged. "<I'll wrap that up for you,>" he said as he went back into the kitchen.

Maou watched him go and let out a light sigh.

"Ain't easy running a nation, huh...?"

Ever since he'd bought a TV for the apartment, Maou had been following the international news far more closely than before. Whenever another country became the topic of discussion, he couldn't help but think about what the world would look like after he was done conquering it. If he ever built the kind of nation he had told Suzuno about by the fire, would the humans living underneath his demon hordes have "food on the table tomorrow"?

"<Here you go,>" said the tavernkeeper, returning with a paper bag and a series of small, tubular objects connected by a string.

"<Just for making the attempt, I'll spot you one of those dumplings for free. And this is one of the firecrackers they set off outside. You're staying with that Church cleric in the inn on the corner, right? I suppose this is kind of a noisy souvenir to bring home, but it's a nice symbol of our country, I think. Go ahead and take it, if it doesn't get in the way.>"

"Hey, Acieth?"

"Oon? What? I need rest before we train..."

"Yeah, that's fine. But you can move, can't you? Let's go on a little digestive walk."

"Okay, but...urp...where?"

Maou gave a strained look to the bag and firecrackers in his hands.

"Out shopping."

✳

"Huh? We go shopping now? ...Erp."

It came as some surprise to Acieth, hands over her ever-so-slightly distended stomach, to see Maou walk right into a general store they had passed by on the street.

"Not like we can do anything else. I don't wanna waste any more time."

"Oooh, if you want...but what is this?"

Maou had selected a shop that apparently dealt in fabrics, traditional handicrafts, and the like. A bit too grandly decorated to be a simple souvenir shop, it mostly featured objects useful in day-to-day life. The mishmash of textiles, clothing, utensils, sculptures, and such that crowded the aisles was reminiscent of a floor in some Tokyo department store.

"But why you want something like this, Maou? Very unusual for you!"

From the shelf, Acieth had picked a small wooden container with a bird-shaped mosaic on the side. It was just small enough that it was hard to picture what it'd be useful for storing.

Next she pointed at a water jug, this with some kind of swan on it. "Do you put gasoline in that?"

"No. Oh, this looks good, though. Could you hold these for me?"

"Oh? ...Huh? Urp."

Acieth gave Maou another quizzical look at what he was holding, as she took the dumplings and firecracker from him.

"I was born very recently, so I don't know, but is that a woman's thing?"

He was carrying a handbag decorated with flowers and birds—two pretty songbirds, sidling up to each other on a branch, along with a happy little slogan written in Yahwan. It wasn't the sort of design Maou would normally be seen sporting.

"I'm not gonna use it, dummy. This is a souvenir. A souvenir."

"Souvenir, souvenir... Oh, a gift?"

"Yeah. For Chi."

"A souvenir for Chiho? I don't want be mean, Maou, but is that important to do now?"

"Hah!" Maou smirked at Acieth as he put the purse back on the shelf. "You, of all people, telling me that. That fancy hairpin is more Suzuno's territory, and it's kind of spendy. That comb could work for Chi, though... Ooh, that costs a lot, too."

He turned to another shelf.

"We have to hold a birthday party once we get back, you know."

"Birthday party?"

"Yeah. For Chi and Emi."

"Really? Emi—my sister merged with her, yes?"

Acieth had never met Emi, but she had heard all about her on the road by now from Maou and Suzuno. Nord, on the other hand, apparently hadn't said much to Acieth about her. Maou had a feeling Emi would have a word or two about that once they were all rescued.

"Yeah. We were supposed to have one a few days before I ran into you and Nord. With everything that idiot Emi's been up to, it's kind of been put on indefinite hold. I've been so busy since then, I haven't made any preparations yet."

It had been a while since the day they had scheduled for the party. It wasn't anyone's fault, and it would have been awkward if he did, but he never got to wish Chiho a happy birthday on the actual day. In fact, on the day of the party, he managed to inadvertently offend Chiho as she fretted over Emi, although Suzuno was kind enough to compliment him for it.

He regretted that, a lot more than he thought he would. And once they had found out where Emi was, he and Suzuno had been so busy preparing for their journey that he'd forgotten to get a present for the party. He had even said so to Chiho's face. Suzuno had every right to call him a villain for that.

"I really don't want to make Chi sad any longer, y'know," he muttered.

He figured Chiho was getting along well enough in Japan, no matter how much the anxiety bothered her. The past few weeks haven't been ideal for them, but once he was back, he wanted to make her smile again.

"...Oh?"

Acieth, watching Maou have a surprising amount of fun picking a gift for Chiho, suddenly felt something was off. She put a hand on her forehead. Her dumpling binge hadn't given her a fever or anything, but when Maou talked about Chiho just now, she had felt this hot flash across her head for a moment. She applied pressure with her fingers for a bit, but the weird feeling didn't go anywhere, so she gave up and shrugged her shoulders.

"So," she said, "that is why you use Suzuno's money to buy present for— *Agh!!*"

Her penchant for honest, pinpoint observations that struck at the heart of Maou's anxieties earned her a reflexive bop on the head.

"I'll pay her back in yen later on!" he nearly shouted.

"Oww, you should stop, Maou... You big violent man... Huh?"

Suddenly, Acieth realized something. Something even more powerful than the aching in her head. She looked up.

"Are you giving present to Emi, too? A female, right?"

"Hmm?"

"You give birthday present to people really important to you, yes? I know Chiho and Suzuno are dear friend to you, but is Emi friend, too?"

"I wouldn't call Suzuno 'dear' to me, exactly, but… Did Nord teach you about birthdays or something, or…?"

He doubted Acieth came to Earth with any knowledge of Japanese birthday customs. Either someone around her talked about it, or she had picked it up from someone in Ente Isla over the past few days when Maou wasn't paying attention.

"I heard about it from Sato. The person who help us. We took our fake name from him."

"Right, right…" Maou sighed and put the carved wooden paper-weight in his hands back on the shelf. "Emi, well; if I'm gonna give Chi a gift, I guess I gotta get something for her, too. Chi would get all pissed otherwise… Well, not pissed, but more like sad or something."

"Ohhh? You give Emi present to make Chiho happy? Weird."

"Well, they're friends, the two of 'em. Or more like Chiho's been trying to make us demons get friendlier with Emi and Suzuno and all that. I mean, as long as I'm in Japan, it won't pay for me to get on their bad side, so if that's what Chi wants, I suppose I oughta think at least a little bit about Emi, too."

"Hmmm," Acieth said, arms crossed with a self-satisfied look on her face. "Women, so hard to understand." But then she suddenly grabbed Maou's arm. "So then, what? What is Emi to you, Maou?"

"Huh. Good question. I mean, there's a lot that's happened, what with Alas Ramus and all, but as a person, she…"

Maou nodded lightly.

"She's my rival, is I guess the best way to put it."

Acieth arched her eyebrows.

"Rival?"

She knew the word, but she probably couldn't comprehend what Maou meant by it. He gave her a bitter smile and headed for the kitchen-utensils section.

"Emi's just as strong as I am; maybe stronger. She knows who I really am, and she's the only person in my life who thinks she's above

me, so to speak. That, and everything I don't have, she's got—but whether she realizes that or not, I dunno. I've been jealous of her more than a few times, y'know? That's why I don't want to lose to her, which is why I'd say 'rival' sums it up pretty well. She keeps on calling me her 'archnemesis' and stuff, too."

"Hmmmmm… But you still give her present on the birthday? Very strange."

Acieth rocked back and forth as she pondered over this. She didn't do so for long, however; she didn't know Emi anyway. So before long, Maou's eyes were back on the merchandise shelves, fixed on another object.

"Hey, what about this?"

He scrutinized it, nestled in among the knives and forks, and realized there were multiple types available.

"This is something you give to people for good luck, I think…"

They were all made of wood, each one carved by hand, often with bird and wing motifs, which was a recurring theme in this shop. But there were also patterns with wineglasses, horseshoes, flowers, stars, and more.

"What do you think of this, Acieth? It's pretty cute, it's useful around the house, and it doesn't take up much space, at least."

"I dunno, but it is good, maybe? …Urp."

With Acieth's perfunctory approval backing him up, Maou decided to go with it. "Chi would like this flowery one," he said. "Emi… These aren't that expensive; I could get one for Alas Ramus, too…and she likes birds, I know. That should work."

So he picked up three of them, his mind more on Alas Ramus than her supposed mother, and brought them to the front counter, confident that he was at least doing something for Chiho over here.

"<Can you wrap up one of these and two of these for me?> All right, Acieth, how's your stomach feeling right… Huh?"

When he turned back around, he realized that Acieth's face had turned white as a sheet. She seemed to have trouble focusing her eyes, her breathing shallow and ragged. Maou, gauging this, began to fear the worst as he picked up the package and stuffed it into a jacket pocket. He wound up having to help Acieth out of the store.

"Hey! Hey, hold it in a little more! You can't do that in the middle of the street!"

But Maou's earnest wish was never to be granted.

"Ooo-*gehhhhhh...*"

"Gaaahhhh!!"

Two things happened at once to make Maou scream in horror. If there was any silver lining to the sordid scene, it's that it didn't take place inside store property.

First, Acieth spewed on top of Maou's shoulders. Her body must have rejected the massive amount she had consumed a bit ago, pushing out everything that had so sorely tested its limits. That made sense. But the bigger problem was that, at almost the exact same time, a beam of purplish light projected out from Acieth's head straight down to the ground.

"Whoa, whoa, whoa!"

The beam was gouging a hole into the surface beneath them, bare earth instead of the concrete of Japan's roads, and it was large enough that Acieth was liable to fall in.

Maou grabbed a strap on her overalls to keep that from happening, but the purple light—whatever physical properties it had—began to hurl both Acieth and Maou, hanging on for dear life, into the air.

"Wha... Huh?!"

He struggled for a better grip, but it was too late. He could see the tavernkeeper from before among the crowd that had quickly gathered around, eyes wide open as he watched the girl rocket into the deep blue yonder. The fact that this spaceship was leaving an arcing path of vomit behind it made the sight no less majestic to the people of Efzahan.

"Hey!" Maou shouted, still hanging from a single strap. "Acieth!! What's going on?! What happened?!"

She just kept groaning, a blank look on her face.

Before long, the scene was chaotic—more evil-banishing fire-crackers going off under them, the local Inlain Crimson Scarves force running to the rescue, and several people on their knees, hands clasped in prayer.

"Wha-wha-wha-what is this, all of a sudden?!"

Nausea was a natural enough symptom for a human being to have. Purple light, on the other hand, was purely a Yesod-fragment thing. Acieth's fragment, just like Alas Ramus's, must have been on her forehead, something Maou had only just discovered with this unexplainable turn of affairs.

But if the fragment was acting up in such sudden, violent fashion, that likely meant just one thing:

"Goddammit… Suzuno and Albert screwed up, didn't they?!"

Alas Ramus was affecting her, from somewhere around the capital. And if the fragment's response indicated whatever was happening to the child, it necessitated exactly that amount of Yesod strength from her sister. And if that's what it was, the only thing Maou could imagine was a powerful, angel-class foe threatening her.

"Acieth! Get yourself together! At least get us back on land and…"

"Urrp."

"H-hey!!"

Acieth, floating in the air, had both hands covering her mouth.

"N-no! Stop! Not this high up…!!"

Despite his concerns for Acieth's dignity—and for the bio-weapon attack about to be unleashed on the crowd below—she somehow managed to hold it in.

Instead, something else came out.

"Aaaaaaagggggggggggghhhhhh…"

The light from her forehead grew even stronger, making Maou unable to let go of her. Like an out-of-control rocket in a tailspin, they hurtled across the city skyline before finally splashing down in a man-made water basin on the outskirts of town.

❊

A few moments before the rocket launch:

"…Not as impressive as I thought it'd be," Emi whispered to

herself as she surveyed Heavensky Keep, visible on the eastern horizon from her hilltop camp in the merchants' quarter.

"What is?"

She turned toward Olba, standing next to her, and shrugged.

"Heavensky. It's always passed itself off as this beautiful castle town that enveloped the very sky itself. And I thought so, too, when I first came here, but looking at it again, it's really not that nice-looking."

"You don't think? Not that I am one to talk, but if Sankt Ignoreido represents the triumph of human civilization on the Western Island, Heavensky plays the same role in the East."

He had a point. Heavensky Keep was a massive castle, one visible from miles around, and the central district that surrounded it was just as vast and majestic. It was like a portrait of a looming mountain spread out before them, but it did nothing to move Emi's heart.

"No, you aren't one to talk, are you?"

The idea of someone who had betrayed the Church and tricked an entire continent into war against a demon race for his own personal gain discussing the beauties of the local scenery disgusted Emi.

"I haven't seen them in real life yet," she continued, "but I've seen pictures and stuff of Kyoto and Himeji Castle when the cherry blossoms are in full bloom in the spring, and... You know, compared to that, this is nothing."

"Hmm. Well, Emilia, if you aren't satisfied with it, you can discuss Heavensky's future direction with the Azure Emperor once you 'rescue' him."

Emi gave Olba the evil eye for a moment, then turned away and headed for her tent in camp. She was due to attend a military conference on the topic of freeing Heavensky, an operation that involved the Hero Emilia's Eastern Island Liberation Army (aka the Phaigan Volunteer Force) plunging into Heavensky's central district and ridding it of the demons that controlled the area.

Olba, of course, was the one who had dragged those Malebranche demons into the Eastern Island in the first place. He had directly worked with them as part of his efforts to bring Emi to Ente Isla and keep her there. And now he wanted to use Emi's power to destroy them.

The volunteers had reached the border between Heavensky's agricultural and merchant districts. Along the way, they had already taken the lives of two Malebranche chieftains. As much as she had craved the heads of the demons—any demon—before she went to Japan, the guilt she felt when she heard that Malebranche leaders Draghignazzo and Scarmiglione were dead was beyond description. It made her look at her hands, recalling how she had once fought just as rabidly against the demons as the Phaigan Volunteers. It made her feel repulsive, ashamed for feeling that way, as she balled her hands into fists.

"*Mommy,*" Alas Ramus said inside her mind, "*what's Kyoto? You mean Tokyo?*"

"...No, it's a big city in Japan. Kind of like Tokyo, but different."

"*Kyoto... Tokyo... Kotyo?*"

She repeated the names a few more times before she got them right. It was enough to rekindle a little warmth in Emi's heart. She fixed the position of the sword she clumsily held on her side and began to walk forward.

At no point in her stay here had she ever deployed her Better Half. Or, for that matter, set off for the front lines and cross swords with any "enemy" at all. It was more convenient for Olba if she was enshrined as the official symbol of the freedom movement, and so long as Emi didn't act too far out of line, he didn't much care what she got up to within the force.

This, at least, meant she never had to unsheathe the holy sword that Alas Ramus materialized for her to kill or maim another creature. By now, however, Olba's motives were a total mystery to her.

As she approached the tent, a harried-looking Eight Scarves knight ran up from his nearby sentry post.

"M-my lady Emilia!"

"What is it?"

"We have word from a vanguard team we deployed to Heavensky in advance. You—you may want to sit down for this!"

"What? Spit it out."

Emi knew it wasn't the Eight Scarves' fault for being dragged into this war, but she couldn't help but be blunt with them anyway. A lot of them were too awed at her noble presence to even say a word to her, but whatever this bit of news was, it must have been worth breaking the ice for.

"This…this is hard for me to believe," the panting messenger reported, "but they said the Great Demon General Alciel was spotted in the main keep of Heavensky!"

The news was just as shocking to Emi. Shocking enough that she totally forgot to use his real name.

"What? Ashiya?!"

"Ashi…?"

"A-Alciel! Was it really Alciel?"

The messenger nodded his head, still unable to believe it himself. "Yes, my lady. The Great Demon General reportedly appeared several days ago. He is commanding the Malebranche, and he's summoned all of the Eight Scarves knights under Heavensky Keep command to prepare for our attack…"

Why was Ashiya in Heavensky? And what for? Emi couldn't even venture a guess. But if Ashiya was here, Emi had just one question to ask.

"What of the Devil King? Is Satan among us?"

It had been her and Suzuno's concern from long before that Maou and Ashiya would be dragged into the Malebranche forces to create a new Devil King's Army. Based on her previous experience, Emi had concluded in the bottom of her heart that such a thing was impossible, but she was nonetheless prepared for the worst.

"Wh-what?" the messenger replied. "N-no, erm, the Devil King? Nothing about that…but did you not defeat him yourself, Lady Emilia?"

That was something Emi picked up on after leaving Phaigan. The exact story behind her current whereabouts differed here and there, but the fact she had defeated Satan, the Devil King, once and for all was taken as settled fact everywhere she went. That must have been what threw off the messenger so badly.

Emi frowned. "I… Yes," she whispered. "Alciel is here, then…" She had no idea why Ashiya would travel to Heavensky by himself, but judging by how harshly he judged the Malebranche's movements, she could presume he didn't volunteer to make the trip. So who had brought him here, and what for?

"Either way…" a voice boomed from behind her, giving her no time to ponder it.

"Ugh…"

"L-Lord Olba…"

"Emilia could make quick work of Alciel by himself. There is nothing to fear. We have no reason to change our strategy."

"I…I imagine not, my lord," the pale-faced messenger said. "Even in the previous battle, Alciel fled to the Central Continent because he was too afraid to face her…"

"…That," a darker-looking Emi said from aside, "is my role, I suppose."

Among all the fighters in the volunteer force, only Emi and Olba had the force required to fight the Demon General on his own terms and have any chance of victory. And while she had no idea what his motives were, if she didn't play the role Olba wanted for her, her dreams would be crushed for good. That much she knew.

"Let us begin, then," Olba said, motioning toward the tent. "We need to work out how we will retake the central district and rescue the Azure Emperor. I think everyone's all here."

The tent was dimly lit, as dark as Emi's own heart, but as she followed behind Olba, a small voice found its way to her mind.

Is Al-cell here?

If anything, Alas Ramus's voice was the opposite of how Emi felt.

If he is, then…

It was practically shining with hope.

…is Daddy, too?

"……Daddy…the Devil King…is…"

Emi's body stiffened, paralyzed in place.

"Mm? What is it, Emilia?" the ever-observant Olba asked. It wasn't enough to rouse Emi from her thoughts.

"...Ah."

What did I think just now? What did Alas Ramus make me think of?

"I..."

There's no way I could be thinking this. There's nothing good that could possibly come of it.

"...I'm sorry, but I need to duck out of this conference. I'm not feeling very good. You just want me to fight whoever's the strongest out of 'em, right? That's fine by me."

With that, Emi turned around, not bothering to wait for a response, and flew out of the tent. "L-Lady Emilia?!" came the voice from the hapless messenger behind her as she quickly dove into her tent and sunk into her simple cot. It was hard to breathe. The palpitations seemed to make noise in her mind.

"What...what is *wrong* with me...?!"

She battered her fists against the bed, almost tearing it apart entirely.

"No matter what... No matter what! I know what he did to me... to my father...!!"

"I've got a whole new world to show you."

The smile on his face, as he related his ridiculous fever dreams to her over that Shinjuku sunset. It all flashed back to her now.

"...You're.........my enemy..."

Whenever Emi's back was against the wall, he'd just waltz in with this huge grin on his face, despite how weak he was. Going on with all that dumb nonsense. And he'd make it all work out in the end.

"Why... Why...?"

"Mommy, Daddy's coming for us! Be good to him, okay?"

She could stand no more.

"...Yeah... Yeah, he will..."

She had no intention of making excuses for her weakened heart, but there was no hiding it any longer. Somewhere, in some cranny of her mind, despite all the sarcasm and whining she spewed over it, she was hoping that Sadao Maou would just waltz on in and rescue both her and everything she held dear.

It wasn't something she wanted to admit. Even now, she thought that entertaining the concept was ridiculous. Emeralda and Albert, her staunchest allies on Ente Isla, had made no moves so far. They must have known something was up, but if even they couldn't do anything about it, how could Maou engineer some miracle from another world? The Idea Link she'd lobbed toward Rika had earned her nothing, and even if she could make contact with her Earth allies, there was no way they'd know what she was dealing with.

But if Ashiya was now on Ente Isla, then Maou must have been on a mad dash to track him down. The moment she thought that, the deepest pit of her heart, the little unshielded bit down there, let out a scream. If Maou followed Ashiya into this world, he would have known what had happened to her. Then he'd come rescue her, too, wouldn't he?

The realization only served to bring an even more miserable thought to the forefront: such an effort would be entirely futile. Solving Emi's problems would involve a lot more than simply grabbing her and Alas Ramus and bringing them back to Japan. The wheat fields her father tended to were far away in the Western Island, and she was unable to give them up. That was why she was plunging herself into this battle she couldn't care less about.

Even if Maou snapped his fingers and reverted to his cloven-hoofed demon form, him versus an Olba-Raguel tag team would be pretty long odds. The moment he did anything to indicate he was protecting Emi, Olba could simply mutter a few words to his men on the Western Island, and then saving her family fields would be physically impossible.

Simply put, unless everyone who knew Emi's backstory disappeared off the face of the planet or people stopped caring about Emilia the Hero entirely, returning to Japan would never grant her the solace she sought. Rumors that Emilia was alive were already starting to filter across the Eastern Island. It wouldn't be long before

Olba used the Eight Scarves to spread the official announcement. And after that, no matter where she fled to, she'd be chased by malicious forces trying to harness her name and her presence.

So what if she simply said "to hell with it," abandoned her father's lands, and settled down in Japan? It would mean nothing. Just as everyone from Lucifer and Suzuno and Sariel to Ciriatto, Farfarello, and Olba did, someone would go over there, lay waste to it without a second thought, and try to capture her anyway. Then she would have to swing her sword against them—to drive back the very Ente Islans she'd sworn to protect.

Every path Emi saw led to despair. No matter what she did, there would be no salvation. But still...

"I hate this...... Why......? How did he get into my heart like this?! Stop screwing with me!"

Now her voice was breaking down into sobs.

She never entertained for a moment the prospect that Ashiya was back here to retake Efzahan or Ente Isla. She knew Maou wouldn't allow that kind of recklessness, and she knew Ashiya would never act without a go-ahead from His Demonic Highness. She knew that because she had spent so much time with them that her heart instinctively told her so.

"Devil...King...!"

She recalled the face of the peppy part-timer from Sasazuka, the guy who seemed to be instantly liked by everybody around him.

"Help...me..."

The tears wouldn't stop coming. She didn't know where her heart lay. It scared her, frustrated her, pained her...and yet the strange sense of relief that it seemed to bring to her kept the tears coming. She fully knew, at that instant, that her identity—her senses of indignation and justice, the things that supported her up to today and drove her to save the world and everyone in it—had just been shattered.

She didn't think it was simply the heartless way Olba and the rest of Ente Isla treated her that made her lose heart. She just never had it in her from the start—that kind of noble will required to bear it all.

"...Eme, Albert...I'm sorry, I'm sorry... Father...I'm sorry, but I can't fight alone anymore..."

Regardless of her birthplace and her blood, Emilia Justina had been just another farm girl enjoying young womanhood until a few years ago. When she wasn't even eighteen, she had gained the will of a Hero through her hatred, and now it was gone.

"I don't know... What should I do...? Father, Eme, Devil King... Please, somebody..."

"Mommy?"

Now Alas Ramus was holding her tearstained face with her warm, silken hands, smiling. She had appeared on top of the bed, through no effort on Emi's part—and for some reason, that crescent shape was on her forehead, as if Emi had summoned her sword or she was picking up on another Yesod fragment. The light, and her smile, were so bright that it seemed to illuminate the muddied darkness in Emi's heart. She clung to her hands.

"Oh... I'm sorry, Alas Ramus, but...I don't think I've got anything else..."

What a pathetic state of affairs. The fact that Alas Ramus's "real" mother was Laila hurt her deeply, and yet all she could do in front of her "daughter" was cry like a baby. But Alas Ramus paid it no heed, her soft skin just as pure as her heart as she spoke.

"I was alone, too."

"...Oh?"

"But now I'm with you, Mommy."

"Alas Ramus...?"

"Mommy, Daddy is always together. Chi-Sis, Al-cell, Suzu-Sis, Luci-fell, Eme-Sis, all together."

Then, for just a moment, Alas Ramus turned away from Emi's eyes. "And A-ceth together, too," she whispered.

"Alas Ramus...?"

"So it's okay. Okay? All back together soon."

"All of us...?" Emi wiped her reddened eyes and let out a quivering sigh. "...Yeah. You're right. I guess we were all together, huh?"

It took that moment for her to realize it. They were enemies, no doubt about that. But over in Japan, it had gone beyond enemies, or demons, or humans. They had spent that whole time together. No matter how "wrong" it was.

"But it can't be that way anymore, Alas Ramus. I didn't notice it until it was too late. The way it is now, even if I gave up on my father's wheat, we can't be together with the Devil King and everyone again."

"Why not?"

"Because..." Emi looked down at her right hand. "Because I didn't want to lose my own dream. So I did what Olba told me...and I killed the Devil King's people."

It wasn't the battle she wanted. The other side wasn't exactly comprised of innocent bystanders, but what Emi was doing now seemed, to her, exactly what the Devil King's Army did to her homeland not long ago. All while she knew that demons were more than just this beastly horde hell-bent on nothing but utter massacre. The Phaigan Volunteer Force was killing Malebranche chiefs who had done nothing wrong, and they were doing so under Emi's name.

It might've been different if she could stand strong and wield her sword in the name of her dreams. But now Emi was immobile, unable to do anything for herself, just sitting there and gauging the situation. The demon-slaying Hero, the supreme commander of all that was good, letting others do the dirty work.

"If there's one thing the Devil King doesn't like," Emi argued, "it's doing anything that violates his code. No matter what kind of excuses I make, he'll never forgive me for acting so selfish like this. I'm sure Alciel wouldn't, either, so..."

She stopped. Suddenly, there was noise coming from outside the tent—soldiers darting to and fro, apparently shouting at each other.

"Ah, Lady Emilia, excuse me," the messenger from before worriedly said to her from beyond the entrance. "A-are you all right? You don't sound well..."

"...I'm sorry. I'm fine."

It was only natural someone would notice all that crying and carrying on. She didn't care much about how she looked to him now, so she simply wiped the sides of her eyes dry and stood up. The light from Alas Ramus's forehead was gone now, and the child was playfully rolling around the bed when the messenger interrupted them.

"I-I apologize," the unnerved knight said, concerned over the streaks still clear upon Emi's face, "but you have been summoned to the military conference. The Great Demon General Alciel has apparently sent us a letter."

"A letter?"

"Yes, my lady. It is addressed to you, I understand, and Archbishop Olba has requested your presence at once."

Emi sniffled a bit, took a deep breath, nodded to herself, and left her tent. It felt too weird to her. How did Ashiya, or Alciel, know she was in this force? The question must have bothered Olba and his generals, for they all looked just as peeved when she entered their tent.

"There you are, Emilia," he greeted her, a sheet of parchment spread out before him.

"That arrived for me? Might I take a look?"

"I suppose we have little choice," Olba grunted. Emi couldn't blame him. Olba knew by now that, over in Japan, "Shirou Ashiya" had been interacting with Emi in a way that went far beyond being friends or foes. His lack of apparent shock at the news of Alciel's return to Ente Isla indicated that he expected as much to happen. Now, though, Olba looked dour, concerned at this new and unanticipated element. He couldn't hide its existence from the Eight Scarves officers, it seemed, but Alciel simply making the move to contact him on Ente Isla was plainly enough to unnerve him.

Olba gave no indication to Emi that he had ever gone to Japan between now and when they had first met again at that mountain in the Western Island. So someone working with Olba (or perhaps Olba himself) must have helped Alciel get back here. And if Olba thought he could control the behavior of Alciel (to say nothing of "Shirou Ashiya"), someone very strong indeed must have been backing him up. It had to be someone among the angels—Raguel was already working with him, after all—but that made it all the more surprising that something allegedly penned by Alciel himself had made it into Emi's hands.

"What is the meaning of this?" Emi said out loud—for much different reasons than Olba and the generals in front of her.

"L-Lady Emilia, please be careful. It is written using a hand we cannot begin to decipher. The very text could be infected with a demonic curse!"

The Eight Scarves leaders were honestly scared, whether they read Emi as feeling the same or not, but either way, they would get nowhere without her reading this. Emi picked up the parchment, cleared her throat, and looked at the text. It began with the Great Demon General Alciel's and Emilia's names in Centurient, and then:

"……Unngh?"

She groaned at what she read. "What does it say?" an irritated Olba asked. For once, she didn't let it bother her.

"Umm… Okay, so there's no demon curse or whatever in here, but you're telling me you couldn't read this, Olba?"

"I know it is the characters of that *other* world," Olba snorted. "An Idea Link can be used well enough for verbal speech, but I did not stay there long enough to understand their entire writing system as well." He pointed at the edge of the parchment. "I can read the phonetic parts of it, the so-called *hiragana*. I know this reads 'bean,' and this reads 'favor.' And between the lines, I can tell he is suggesting that he seeks revenge."

"Well…you aren't wrong, but…"

Emi nodded at Olba's roundabout guessing and looked back down at the message. Alciel was trying to tell her something with this. And she could tell, somehow, that Alciel had no intention of actively engaging her in combat. But what was the crux, the core message he was giving her? That made no sense.

"What does it say, my lady?! I hardly expect that Alciel wishes to send a package to you next?"

"N-no, I don't think it's that, but…"

Emi's mind raced. Ashiya had to have chosen these words for a good reason. What was he trying to say?

"Well then, what?!"

"Uhmm… Well, hang on, I really don't know, either. What reason could he have for this…?"

All this consternation was chiefly thanks to the main body of the text, which read, in its entirety and with Ashiya's neat handwriting, as follows:

I promise you the cold tofu and ginger favor will be returned.

"Just tell me what is written on the paper, then," Olba continued.

"Ermm," Emi meekly began, "this says 'cold tofu' here. Tofu's this food that they make from soy milk."

A single look informed Emi that this was not the explanation the tense array of officers in front of her was hoping for.

"To-fu? What is this *to-fu*?"

Well, it's good in miso soup. Emi almost caught herself saying it, stopping herself just in time.

"Um, I don't know how I could put it in a way you'd understand, but it's this soft, white kind of food that comes in these blocks the size of a small brick, and it's kind of jiggly because of all the water in it, and it…doesn't really taste like anything, but…"

".T-taste?!" one of the Eight Scarves generals shouted. "Are you telling me the people of this other world actually *eat* such a bizarre thing?!"

"B-bizarre? Well, maybe it is, but…"

Then something caught in Emi's mind. She had heard that combination somewhere before. Something that only she would ever understand. In fact, she had eaten it at one point. It was the classic problem of being unable to remember what you had for lunch two days ago, and it frustrated her as she continued speaking.

"But this word, 'ginger,' it's this herb that grows in these purplish-red bulbs, and when you bite down on it, it's really bitter and, like, goes right up into your nose…"

"Hmph. A fearsome, devilish weed, this sounds like."

"Such mystic and inscrutable things these alien creatures consume…"

A fairly negative response, one partially instigated by Emi's lack of cooking-show-host skills. She just didn't know which Ente Islan foods to compare this stuff to, and it was costing her. She soldiered on, pantomiming a knife-chopping motion.

"So you cut this ginger up into tiny pieces, and you put it on top of the chilled tofu, and…oh."

Then her mind went back in time to that cramped dining table in an old, beat-up apartment building, one that seemed so oddly attractive to her now, to the point that she thought of little else. There, before her eyes, was Maou, acting so finicky about his dinner that he shoved the ginger on his plate on top of Emi's own tofu.

"Emilia, what is it?"

"…!"

Emi snapped out of it. The generals were looking on, worried, but Emi paid them no heed. Her heart was trembling, for different reasons than from those back in her tent. Her cheeks reddened, and she felt a burning sensation behind her eyes and in the pit of her stomach. Now she knew what Alciel was trying to say—and the moment she realized it, an indescribable sense of relief and happiness spread over her, one strong enough to catch her off guard.

Just a few minutes ago, she had thought her hopes were futile. She had resigned herself to the fact that a certain chapter of her life was over, and a new one had irrevocably begun. But now, before her eyes, that was being transformed into hope once again.

"O-Olba…"

But she still kept her mind sharp, preventing the rolling stone of her emotions from gathering any more momentum down the hill.

"Wh-what?" The dismay was now clear upon Olba's face.

"There's no time left to lose. We must head for Heavensky at once."

"I…I beg your…?"

"We have to move fast, or whether you or I want it or not, Ente Isla is going to be enshrouded in darkness once more. Alciel has a secret plan in motion—one he believes gives him a chance against me, even at his full powers. He's using coded Japanese words to tell us to pull back our forces if we want to live."

"You…you are sure of this?" Olba offered, unable to too strongly question the Hero in front of the Eight Scarves brass.

"It is true," Emi resolutely countered, unsure where this line of conversation was taking her. "If he puts this 'cold tofu' and 'ginger' together, he can obtain the kind of power that outclasses the likes of the Great Demon General Lucifer—or even the Devil King himself!"

"Wh-what?"

And the thing was, Emi wasn't lying.

"And this combination," she whispered into Olba's ear as the rest of the conference descended into chaos, "was what Alciel used before my very eyes to turn the tables on Satan. He very nearly felled me in the process, and you know how serious that could be."

"It… It cannot be…"

"That was one big reason why I came back here from Japan all of a sudden. If I hadn't dodged the 'ginger' that wound up hitting home with Satan, who knows where I'd be right now? <And,>" she continued, switching to Japanese so the Eight Scarves wouldn't understand her, "<you and Lucifer obtained demonic powers in Japan, right? Well, there's another type of energy that exists in that world; one that we didn't know about, but Alciel found it! A power stronger than demonic force itself, one capable of overwhelming the once-invincible Devil King. Tofu—and ginger!>"

Now Olba, at least, knew what Emi was really getting at. And, again, there was not a single embellishment to it. It was the truth, albeit a fairly one-sided take on it.

"You…you must be mistaken…!"

"<I don't know what you're scheming to do, but whatever it is, you better hurry up with it before it's too late. Make light of Alciel's powers right now, and not even I might make it out alive.>"

"Khh… So be it!" Olba turned around and began giving orders to his generals.

It was clear to Emi that Olba intended to send her up to bat against Alciel and his forces in Heavensky. But Emi was the only one who understood this letter, something that doubtlessly filled Olba with anxiety. A master strategist like Olba knew all too well how a single uncertainty could make even the most solid of expectations burn to ashes. She fixated upon his back, wiping off a tear that made it through her mental barrier.

"I guess," she said to herself, "he was good for something more than standing in line multiple times to stock up on 'limit one per customer' eggs."

She still had no idea how he got the letter through to her, but she had to hand it to his acuity and originality: A single sentence was all it took to completely turn her situation around. Right now, in this world, there was only one person who could "return" the tofu-and-ginger favor.

"The Devil King... He's coming."

Who else could repay the favor? It was Maou. The one who had spooned that ginger on top of Emi's tofu in the first place. Emi crossed her arms to keep a budding smile from erupting on her face.

It wasn't like anything was solved. Even if Maou regained his demon form and fought alongside her, her father's wheat field was still under Olba and Raguel's control, liable to be torched at any minute. But now her vision, previously shut away by dark despair, seemed to shine more brightly than ever before. Was she just kidding herself?

She was sure that, if Maou really was coming, he wouldn't simply rescue Ashiya and leave her here. She had to believe that; every single time before, he'd never done anything like abandon her, no matter how much he might have bitched and moaned about it. And no matter how much he hated Emi, he really did love Alas Ramus. But more than that, if Maou was really willing to leave Emi on the side of the road, Ashiya would have no reason to send her a missive suggesting otherwise.

There was no telling what would come next. She might not have realized it, but at that moment, Emi, in her own away, had abandoned her father's field, her peaceful life in Japan, and everything

else in her life. In other words, she abandoned thinking about any-thing that would come after Maou appeared. Her dreams, the fate of the old wheat field, everything about the "Emi Yusa" she had left behind in Japan—she stopped dwelling on any of it.

She had no idea when Maou would be there, or when he would take action. She had no clue about anything. And if she didn't, she knew she had to keep dancing on the palms of Olba and his cronies behind the scenes for now. Even if their hands got tired and they put them down, she had to keep going. And she had to keep pushing at it, in order to make sure the unexpected appearance of the real "hero" produced the most explosive climax possible.

"Guess I'm too stupid to come up with any better ideas," she laughed to herself. Strangely, it didn't sound as self-deprecating as she thought it would. It was exactly what she felt, straight from the bottom of her heart—and that's what must have made it feel so bright and refreshing. Alas Ramus, inside her, apparently picked up on that.

"Mommy? Feel better?"

"…Yeah. I think I do, kind of."

The whole line of thinking, she knew, was pretty selfish of her. That's why, if everything actually worked out and they were all around that warm dinner table again:

"They're never gonna let me hear the end of it. In fact, maybe it'll make us enemies for good this time. But still…"

She'd have to leave the past behind and honestly apologize for the past week. She was ready to commit on that.

THE HERO DANCES ON THE BATTLEFIELD

Amid the chill yet supremely awkward atmosphere, Albert glared at the dust around his feet as he followed Suzuno.

"Hey," he said, "did you know there was someplace like this in Heavensky?"

"I had some intelligence on it, yes."

"Intelligence... Oh, that?"

"I am part of the 'fanatical dark side,' remember? You know just as well as I do, Albert, that half the missionaries serve as secret agents sent out by Sankt Ignoreido, unafraid to stake their lives for the sake of our god. So they do just that, risking their necks to send intelligence back to the capital."

"Yeah, but man, talk about a find! How much time and manpower does it take to do something like this?"

The two of them were walking down an underground passage—and not a normal one. It was part of the catacombs, the subterranean passageways that served both as crypts for the dead and as alternate paths beneath the castle walls that crisscrossed Heavensky all the way out to the agricultural districts. Under the light of the magical illumination Suzuno had crafted from her hands, the path was quiet, immobile and frozen in time except for the dust they were kicking up.

"In case of a national emergency, the Azure Emperor is to be taken through a specific route in these catacombs to the Cloud Retreat in Heavensky. It has never been used for that, but the Regal Azure Scarves have all their stations underground in here, in order to keep them classified and ready if the worst happens."

Albert shrugged as he followed Suzuno, who was keeping a close eye on her surroundings as she unerringly navigated the twisting passages.

"Funny to think of a Church official talking about 'classified' information from Efzahan and all that."

Suzuno nodded in agreement. "Well, the entire idea behind it is a farce. If the Azure Emperor was actually forced to use these crypts to escape, it would mean the empire of Efzahan was essentially no more. If he would ever willingly abandon the capital of an empire so rife with the seeds of conflict as this one, his power would crumble in an instant. That is both the reason why these catacombs must exist, and why they must never see actual use. Thus, their existence is both classified and out in the open. Parts of the network are even visited by tourists in search of the tombs of the pre-Efzahan kings."

"Ooh, yeah, I heard about that. Some of the passages under the eastern walls are giant graves for the old dynasties 'n' things, right? Is that what we're in? Whether it's a public secret or not, if we can get in this easily, wouldn't this be a perfect base for rebels?"

"Indeed. That is why the Regal Azure Scarves, the group closest to the emperor, is responsible for managing them."

They had entered this catacomb through an Eight Scarves station on the dividing line of the capital's merchant district. One wouldn't normally expect that to serve as an access point for the general public, but the soldiers normally securing the checkpoint weren't there at all, leaving it wide open. It couldn't have been a trap—there were over a hundred of these stations lining the walls in Efzahan, and considering Heavensky was still unaware of them, the idea of contriving such an elaborate ruse for an enemy they didn't know to exist seemed impossible.

"And that is only the Regal Azure Scarves," Suzuno continued.

"Soldiers ranked Inlain Jade or below, even if they are aware of the catacombs, would never know the correct route to the Cloud Retreat."

Although known collectively as the Eight Scarves, the knights in Efzahan's service were subject to a strict pecking order. The Regal Azures up top, and the Inlain Crimsons on the bottom, were often so far removed from each other that even conversation between them was taboo.

"Wait," a confused Albert interjected. "So how do you know the way, then? I don't care how many moles you Church people have; if only the Regal Azures know about this..."

He was stopped by an icy stare Suzuno shot him over her shoulder. No longer was this the friendly Suzuno Kamazuki whom Emilia relied upon in Japan.

"You cannot see it, Albert?" said the former highest-ranking official in the Council of Inquisitors, the tyrant known as the Scythe of Death. She flashed a light smile, turned back around, and kept going. "Exactly when these passages were built underneath this metropolis, I cannot say. But tread along the same paths for a few hundred years or so, and they will start to look quite rutted to you."

"Oh?"

"It would be quite unlikely to have concrete information on pathways that were never meant to be discovered. But look around us. It is much safer to use magic-driven illumination in caverns like these instead of fire—the Regal Azure forces are packed with talented sorcerers. And if a pathway's been lit by magical light over years and years, it could hardly be easier for me to spot it."

"...Well, huh. Impressive."

It was then that Albert realized that Suzuno's feet were making no sound whatsoever as she moved. He could only hear his own footsteps echoing in the chamber. It reminded him all over again that this was no rank-and-file Church cleric he was traveling with.

After a moment, something else occurred to him:

"So how come we aren't seein' any Regal Azure men in here?"

"..."

"There's gotta be some people in the volunteer force who're high up enough in nobility to know the way through here. They might even use this path to stage their attack. And whether the Razures left in Heavensky are gonna side with them or with Alciel, the fact is that there ain't a soul down here besides us. You don't find that odd?"

"Indeed. I do not know the reason for it…but if you think about it, the Eight Scarves post we used to access these catacombs was empty as well. Ever since I set foot in Efzahan, those forces have been acting rather strangely in my eyes. Soldiers are not posted where they should be. Instead they are being sent away from the capital, into the outlying areas where they are hardly needed."

Suzuno recalled the Regal Crimson Scarves patrol she ran into on the way to Honpha.

"The capital has to know by now that the volunteer force is coming for them. They must have a reason to position their forces where they are. Whatever it is, it certainly suits our needs right now. We need to take full advantage of it."

She floated her light ahead of her a bit and let out a soft groan.

"If we can see the goal in front of us, we need to keep pressing forward. Even if it lands us in the tiger's den."

"Yeah…"

Presently, the two came upon an enormous gate that was just ever-so-slightly ajar, like a predator hiding its fangs. Beyond it was a stairway that extended upward to parts unknown. They paused for a moment to scope it out. No demons or Regal Azure soldiers were about.

"Let's go. Do not fall behind me."

Dimming her light down to a faint glow, Suzuno shot up the stairs like a gust of wind, ascending its full length in short order. Albert faithfully followed, although the lack of traps or guards along this stairway that seemed to go on for hundreds of steps unnerved him. Once they were up, they were in another corridor, lightless and of the same build as where they'd come from. It wasn't a very long one, and on the far end was a plain, unadorned wall.

"You think that's a revolving door or somethin'?"

"No. Above us. Lend me your shoulder for a moment, Sir Albert."

"Above us? …Whoa, wait a minute!"

Without bothering to wait for a reply, Suzuno hopped up and planted her feet squarely on Albert's shoulders.

"Is this what 'lending a shoulder' means in Japan?" Albert complained as Suzuno peered at the ceiling.

"It is so helpful to have a man helping me at times like these."

"I ain't a stepladder, y'know! What're you even doing?"

Albert tried to look up at Suzuno's hands, her flowing robes guarding him from any accusations of peeping.

"Keep your legs braced."

"Huh? Erf…!"

Suddenly, he felt a great weight upon his shoulders.

"Nnhh… Oof!"

Suzuno's heels dug into him. He did his best to stand strong, and as he did, Suzuno let out a low grunt of effort that didn't seem to match her light form at all. The dust around Albert's feet lifted into the air, and then light began to come down from the ceiling.

"…Ah. So the entrance to the hidden passage was in the ceiling, then, not the wall?"

"It seems to be the case, yes. Lift me up, could you? Then I will pull you up."

As instructed, Albert pushed Suzuno's body above his head. In a moment, she had an arm dangling down to pick him up—something she did with seemingly no effort, despite how thin her limbs were.

Once he was through, Albert found himself in a fairly roomy chamber that seemed to be a sort of changing room. It was dark, simply because it was dark outside—Suzuno and Albert had been underground for most of the day. Still, thick candles were all they had to gauge the room with. There were mirrors on the wall, oaken chairs with ornate designs on them carved by some master woodworker, and a separate small dresser with a mirror on top. The walls featured paintings of natural scenes done in brilliant pigments and even a bit of gold leaf. Anyone would assume that the room belonged to someone in nobility. The light, sweet smell that pervaded the air might have been perfume, or incense.

"What kind of room is this, then?"

Albert was hardly lowborn, but he had never been one for luxury, either. He asked the question out of sheer curiosity, then quickly regretted it.

"A privy, I would imagine."

"A...what?"

He looked down at the hand he had just used to touch the floor earlier.

"Like a toilet?"

"Seems so."

Albert started looking around the room, suddenly flustered. "Well... Well, I dunno much about how the nobility around here live, but how could anyone relax in a bathroom as big as this one? And...um, where would they do it?"

He had assumed it was a changing room or something, but no—it was a bathroom. And it seemed to be lacking the one thing any bathroom needs.

"...Is it that thing?"

He looked to Suzuno for confirmation as he pointed at an object in the corner, a box-shaped silver compartment situated lower than the rest of the room.

"Pure silver, if I had to guess," Suzuno reported. "I could hardly imagine the work and expense to keep that clean. Alciel would be shocked."

"What's a secret passage doing in here, though...?"

"When you are building a castle, it is vital that only a limited number of people know where the secret passages are. That is why you often find them in baths, or privies, or within the sewers—areas where extra space next to a room would not raise any eyebrows on the blueprints, but are never accessed on a regular basis."

"Well, yeah, but how many people are gonna be opening up the floors of their bathrooms, normally?"

"The passage below us is connected by the ceiling instead of a revolving door in order to trick intruders into believing they have reached a dead end, I would imagine. There might have been another exit elsewhere besides this one, of course, but this is the path we have found, I suppose."

"Oof... Rough."

Albert couldn't articulate exactly what was rough, but that was the only way he could put his feelings into words.

"Nothing to worry about. This privy is obviously meant for nobility. Hardly the kind of thing peasants in the Western Island would use. I am sure the floor is polished regularly."

"Yeah, I hope so."

Albert gave another sad look at his palms as Suzuno put her ear on the door leading out of the room.

"Hmm."

"What is it?"

"...Rather strange place, this."

"Strange?"

"I am detecting a large amount of demonic force, right alongside a barrier of holy magic. Do you feel anything a little above your head?"

"Hmm..." Albert looked at the ceiling, closed his eyes, and quickly nodded. "Oh, you're right. Wanna check it out?"

"I doubt it is Alciel, but demonic force and a holy barrier so close together have to be there for a reason. It would be worth examination."

"True, but we're definitely gonna be runnin' into some Eight Scarves or Malebranche guys now, yeah? What're we gonna do about—"

"Ah!'

"Ahh!"

"...Oh."

With no warning whatsoever, the door to the privy opened. Two men entered, bolts of deep green cloth wrapped around their arms identifying them as Regal Jade Scarves. They had cleaning equipment in their hands, and the sight of Suzuno and Albert clearly gave them pause. They weren't expecting the room to be occupied, and Suzuno had been too preoccupied with the twin magical forces nearby to spot them.

"""""   """"""
......

They looked at each other, shocked into silence, but only for a few seconds.

"Well! Nice to see how clean it was in the end, yes?"

"Yeah, but I still feel kinda bad for 'em…"

"You should be more thankful. Now we know where the Azure Emperor's Cloud Retreat is, am I right?"

There was a twinge of regret to Suzuno's and Albert's voices as they boldly ran their way down a Cloud Retreat hallway.

The two Regal Jade soldiers had been left behind to take care of the emperor himself, and the privy was one of several that only the emperor was allowed to use (the fact he had several exclusive johns was a further surprise for Albert).

Despite the circumstances, the emperor was too important to leave by himself, so several Regal Azure and Regal Jade men were still serving as his personal guard, even as the Malebranche took over the castle. Only the Razure were authorized to wait on and guard the emperor himself, however; Regal Jades were forbidden from even coming near him, so they occupied the time by maintaining his chambers and household equipment.

"Has to be a pretty crappy job, though," Albert whispered, eyebrows furrowed downward. "Hope they transfer somewhere better once things calm down a bit."

With as clear and insurmountable a hierarchy as the one the Eight Scarves had established for themselves, and with the sense of pride the Regal Jades seemed to have at being their leader's official toilet scrubbers, Albert couldn't help but feel pity for them.

"I am sure," Suzuno countered, "that their opinion of their current post is why they told us where the Azure Emperor was. We were clearly trespassing, but they decided helping us was still better than leaving the castle in the hands of demons. They deserve a royal commendation, if anything."

The troops had ordered the two intruders to identify themselves, but it was clear in their voices that their hearts weren't in it. They were clearly exhausted, and when Albert gave his name, one of them recognized his face—the face of the past liberator of the Eastern Island. That eliminated any threat that it'd come to blows, and the Regal Jades believed Albert when he had said they were here to rescue the emperor. They gave a verbal description of the Cloud Retreat's layout, and then they ripped up their jade armbands, cutting each one into three ropes of fabric that Suzuno and Albert could use to avoid combat with other Eight Scarves men. Two ropes went on the left arm, one went on the right—an arrangement that, in the signaling language of the Eight Scarves, meant the wearer was an ally.

"They did say something interesting, though…"

"Oh?"

One of the men had stated that the Regal Azure and Regal Jade forces had been "left behind" to serve the Azure Emperor. This meant that, behind the scenes, the forces that hadn't been left behind had been ordered to go somewhere else. And in a Heavensky Keep that was crawling with angels, Malebranche, and a Great Demon General, it seemed hard to believe that the emperor had any direct managerial control over the Eight Scarves by this point. So who had the power to control the Eight Scarves men who weren't part of the volunteer force—men still under Heavensky influence?

"…No," Suzuno said. "Now is not the time to think about that. The emperor should be at the other end of those stairs. I feel a powerful barrier of holy magic. Let's go!"

Things seemed to be going a little too well at this point. But if they could secure the Azure Emperor, all they had to do then was make a beeline for the main volunteer force base. Staying undercover wouldn't matter at that point. The Phaigan forces' primary mission was to release the emperor from demonic influence, and that naturally meant ensuring he was safe. If Suzuno could accomplish that, it would at least buy them some more time before hostilities between the volunteer and capital forces began in earnest.

"What…is this?"

At the top of the stairs, Suzuno and Albert found a large, broad room—a chamber, really, one far more ornately decorated than even the privy they had climbed into earlier. A room literally fit for a king. The lack of furnishings for entertaining visitors or holding royal hearings indicated this was likely a private room.

It contained a bed gigantic enough to house ten grown adults, and when Suzuno spotted the figure lying on it, she stiffened her posture a bit. This was the Azure Emperor, nothing more than a strategic presence in her mind up to now, but he was still the leader of a nation. It was no one Albert or Suzuno would normally ever have the right to see in person, and regardless of what they personally thought of him, they would have to approach him with the utmost respect.

"<Your Highness,>" Suzuno began in carefully worded Yahwan, "<please forgive my rudeness in invading your private bedchamber.>"

There was no response.

"<…? Your Highness…?>" Suzuno took a step forward.

"Wait."

Albert stopped her with a hand to her shoulder.

"That ain't the Azure Emperor."

"What?"

"Plus, where's the holy-magic barrier? I thought there was supposed to be one around the room, around the bed—"

He failed to finish the sentence. Before he could, the air around both them and the bed suddenly began to warm and dim.

"Well, well, who is this? You have quite the impudence, invading the emperor's personal bedroom."

""—?!""

Faster than anyone could notice, Suzuno removed her hairpin. Albert joined her, balling his fists into a fighting stance. But the figure that appeared from the swirling black took its time to stroll forward, apparently uninterested in a fight. She looked at the twisted, one-armed figure, then gasped.

"L-Libicocco?!"

"...Ah. You, eh?"

She knew this demon. In fact, they had just met about a week ago, Church cleric Suzuno against Malebranche chieftain Libicocco, in the air above Chiho's high school in Sasazuka.

"You know him, Bell?"

"...I do," a clearly surprised Suzuno replied. Libicocco, watching her, seemed far less perturbed. "You had been dealt a grave injury... by human standards. Feeling better now, it looks like?"

"...What about you? You can hardly be healed up yet."

It was somewhat odd for two fighters who had engaged in life-or-death combat a week ago to worry about each other's well-being. But Suzuno was fine. Her massive slash wound was now just a red mark that didn't hurt at all. Chiho could hardly believe it herself.

Libicocco, on the other hand, was still missing the arm that Maou had removed with his sword. It was entirely possible, Suzuno figured, that some of the demon races could grow back missing parts like so many lizard tails—but here, on Ente Isla, the demonic force he projected seemed much weaker to Suzuno than what he had wielded at Sasahata North High.

"Strangest thing," the demon said. "The wound stubbornly refused to close itself, for the longest time. Treatment with dark force seemed to do nothing. And so here I am, away from the front lines, working the kind of guard duty that any human could do." He eyed Suzuno and Albert again. "And who is that man with you? Whoever he is, he's clearly possessed with more than his fair share of holy force. I was told to expect you, but nobody like him."

"What?"

The observation set off alarm bells in Suzuno's mind, but she wasn't thrown for long. "Begone, Libicocco," she shouted. "You know as well as I do that staying here in Efzahan will do nothing to restore the Devil King's Army."

"…"

"The Phaigan Volunteer Force led by Emilia the Hero is taking over Malebranche-controlled lands, village by village, city by city. Soon, they will be at the door of Heavensky Keep. Remaining in this castle will provide you with nothing but a needless death."

Libicocco fixed his eyes on her, still silent.

"This was doomed from the start, and you know it! Though it may be difficult for your kind to accept, the Malebranche have been tricked by Olba Meiyer and the archangels. They have fallen straight into a trap set by the heavens. Do you think the Devil King wishes all of you to fritter away your lives? It is not too late, Libicocco. Call your forces back and return to the demon realms. Tell Alciel the same as well. He is hardly slow enough not to understand the situation."

"…"

"Libicocco!"

"I am aware. I am fully aware, all right? I know that we were idiots. I know that Raguel and that Olba man were fishy from the start. But you know what? There is no turning our backs to this."

"Raguel? Not another angel…" Suzuno winced at the unexpected name. Fighting against Gabriel and Camael was hopeless enough, but adding another angel to the mix meant she and Albert couldn't afford to waste another second. The angels would seek to eliminate anyone and anything in the way of their plans, so standing around here in the Cloud Retreat, playing verbal tennis with a demon, was a dangerous waste of precious time.

"Perhaps not," she offered, "but that does not mean you lack the power to end this! All you have to do is hand the Azure Emperor over to the Phaigan forces and return to the demon realms! That is all it takes to keep you from wasting your lives. The Devil King Satan refused to punish Ciriatto for his crimes! He would doubtlessly be just as—"

"That's not the problem, woman. You don't understand any of this."

"What?"

"When I say there's no turning our backs, I'm not talking about our current situation. I'm talking about the ideals of the original Devil King's Army."

"The ideals?"

He meant, Suzuno presumed, the tenet that the people of the demon realms should never have to starve. Maou had stated it himself. But what point was there to bringing that up at a time like this?

"As Lord Alciel described it to us, this is our first, last, and only chance to give our demon tribes a chance to survive in the future. And now you are meddling in that. Perhaps you can understand our resulting...frustration."

"What are you saying? Do you actually think Alciel wants the angels to take advantage of you in their conquest of Efzahan?"

Libicocco's phrasing gave Suzuno pause. There was no way Ashiya could have overlooked the ones pulling the strings behind all this. He'd been kidnapped by Gabriel himself!

But the way Libicocco seemed to be putting it, Ashiya, or Alciel, was in command of Heavensky. Which meant he was the one moving Eight Scarves forces around?

"That is not for me to know," the demon replied. "It is Lord Alciel's order, and so shall it be. There is only one in this world allowed to go past this room. If anyone else dares to attempt it..."

Libicocco took his eyes off the stunned Suzuno. It took her a few moments to understand why.

"Wh-whoa!!"

Ignoring Albert's plea, Suzuno summoned her Light of Iron and bore down on Libicocco with her gigantic warhammer.

"Okay, time out, folks..."

She was an instant too late.

"Ngh...?!"

Several instants, actually. Because her hammer was now stopped cold against a single bare palm—and not Libicocco's.

"My, my—good work, good work, team. I don't know how you got all the way in here without anyone noticing, but you definitely have come a long way. And without any bullet trains or anything, even."

"Wh-who the hell are you?!" Albert shouted. Before the person himself could answer, Suzuno revealed the detestable truth.

"Gabriel...?!"

The archangel, looking just as arrogant as ever, looked more astonished to see Albert in the room than Suzuno.

"Hmm? You're someone from here, aren't you? One of Emilia's allies? What happened to the Devil King?"

"We have nothing to say to you!"

"Now, now. Not that I can blame you, but that's awfully mean. But, still, you should be glad it's me who popped up here. You're, uh, Libicocco, right? I saw you sent an Idea Link straight in my direction—did you get word from Alciel or something?"

"..."

"Ngh...?!"

The demon must have taken his eyes off of Suzuno to focus on casting some dark magic. But it made little sense to her; why would Libicocco, who knew all along he was being deceived by the angels, be told by Alciel to tell Gabriel, of all people, all about Suzuno's presence? The doubt must have been written clearly on her face, because Gabriel grinned widely at her.

"Now, I'm sure you all have pleeenty of your own questions, but if you do, d'you mind asking Alciel about them once we're all done here? Assuming you're in any position to reach him, of course."

"Wh-what?! Mngh!!"

"Gah! Wh-wha...?!"

All Gabriel did was move one of his fingers a little. That was all it took to freeze both of them on the spot—Suzuno still holding her hammer, Albert's fists still ready to strike.

"In any event, I would really appreciate it if you all didn't meddle; we're just getting to the good stuff. If we're gonna do this right, we need everyone here at just the right moment, y'know?"

"What...are you...?!"

"Hrrrnnngh...!"

Struggle as they did, neither Suzuno nor Albert could even twitch.

"You guys can come on back once the gang's all here. After that, you can do whatever you want with the old emperor livin' high on the hog upstairs. That, and Emilia's father, sleeping over there."

"Ah...?!"

Neither of them could turn their heads. They strained their eyes to the far corners of their sockets, training them on the bed across the room.

"Well, I'm out. Dunno when we'll meet again, but keep it real, mm-kay?"

And that was all the time Gabriel provided them. Suddenly, the scene began to vastly change. The endlessly irritating archangel, the Malebranche chieftain rubbing his head in frustration, the Cloud Retreat, the man on the bed, and everything else in their sight spun like a revolving kaleidoscope as Suzuno and Albert were thrust into another dimension.

"Wh-what are we...?!"

"Dammit, it's a Gate!"

It was. And it swallowed them the next instant. Suzuno attempted to right herself, but the aftereffects of the petrifying spell made it a slog. The torrential speed at which Gabriel's Gate was propelling them made it impossible to resist the flow in any useful manner.

"God...damn it...!!" Suzuno shouted out in frustration. *What a state of affairs*, she thought. Now she was here, her body being jostled and jarred by a power she was helpless to defy.

"Look out! Here comes the exit!!"

"...! What?!"

Suzuno wiped the outer corners of her eyes and turned her head toward Albert.

This was too fast. It hadn't even been a minute since they were thrown in. So they weren't going to Earth, *or* another world?

"I don't know where we're landing! Watch out!"

Suzuno didn't need to be told twice. She balled herself up, preparing for whatever awaited her. Soon, she saw light pour out from the other side of the exit:

"…A city?"

"We're coming out!!"

The world suddenly regained its color. Air filled the space around them, and instead of the unstoppable torrent of the Gate, the warm sun greeted them. They had been tossed into the air, but they were still low enough that they could clearly see the people below them.

It looked like a pretty large town. The Gate exit's opening and closing must have disturbed the air around them, because an approaching flock of pigeons suddenly changed their flight pattern to dodge Suzuno.

The sound of a bell filled her ears.

Something was wrong. She had left Maou alone just a few hours ago. Efzahan was supposed to be dark right now!

From the corner of her eye, Suzuno checked the position of the sun. It made her gasp. This couldn't be…

"Hey! Can you fly?!" Albert, not noticing Suzuno's confusion, pointed downward. "There's a big building over there with a flat roof! I'm gonna land on it!"

The sight of the building, along with the town around it, confirmed Suzuno's worst suspicions.

""—!""

The two of them summoned their holy energy to glide gently downward. Albert had spotted the building quickly enough to make landing on it a fairly simple task. But Suzuno was still clearly flustered—and when Albert dusted himself off and looked around, he quickly had the same questions Suzuno did.

"Is this…"

Albert fell silent as he surveyed the city below him. When he spoke again, as he eyed an even larger building far away, his voice was shaking.

"S-Saint Aile…?"

"It has to be."

Suzuno gritted her teeth. *Here*, of all places.

Right in front of them loomed Castle Ereniem, the massive fortress that served as the Empire of Saint Aile's center of government.

In a way, this was far worse news than being sent to some alien world. They were now on the opposite side of the planet from Heavensky. Suzuno couldn't open a Gate without a suitable amplifier; if she wanted to return to Heavensky, her only choice was to use the so-called Stairs to Heaven—the nearest of which was in a prelate site on the far western edge of Saint Aile's capital. That was a good two days on horseback from Ereniem, and Suzuno and Albert didn't have days to waste on travel any longer.

They were at the end of their rope, and Suzuno knew it. She fell to her knees there, on the roof of the Church temple upon which they had landed, and used a shaky hand to remove a cell phone from her robe. The only thing she had the power to do now was call up Maou and explain this sorry state of affairs to him—but he was useless at the moment, and she would essentially have to ask him to deal with three angels at the same time.

"My god..."

She balled her fists like a frustrated child, helplessly pounding one of them against the temple roof.

"Whoa, wait a minute! Wait a minute. This might be better for us than we thought."

"...What?"

"If that's Castle Ereniem over there, that means we're in the Oreus District right now. Which means... Yeah, there it is! The Holy Magic Administrative Institute."

"The Holy... You mean where Lady Emeralda is? W-wait, Oreus? In that case, we have to be standing on..."

Suzuno looked down at the roof she'd been beating her fist against a moment ago. Her eyes opened wide.

"Right," Albert said. "And if my memory ain't failing me, we're on the Cathedral of Oreus in Saint Aile's main diocese, where the trials were held."

The cleric could feel the strength return to her legs. There was still hope. If they could pull this off, they might be back in Heavensky very, very soon.

Albert, looking back at her, nodded deeply.

"Eme's right under our feet at the moment."

✳

A howling wind began to blow as dark clouds encircled the air above Heavensky. Gabriel watched them from his post atop a wall extending out from the keep. The sight of the moon, peeking out between the ominous clouds, made him smile.

"Well, that settles it. Whether they were lookin' out for it or not, nothing that's about to happen to this city right now will be seen by anyone."

The words dashed themselves against the wind, escaping the notice of anyone else.

"It's the Hero Emilia versus Alciel, general of the New Devil King's Army. The entire cast of characters, right here onstage! That's what you're thinking, isn't it? Well, sucks to be you, mm-kay? Just sit back and enjoy one hell of an unscripted drama."

Gabriel gave a self-satisfied nod as he looked over the northern outer reaches of Heavensky.

"If life's too easy for these humans, they just kind of fall apart, ya know? You gotta keep 'em frantic, or it's no good. After all, we're living, breathing beings, too."

✳

"What...could this be?" The Phaigan Volunteer Force general taking the lead stiffened his voice. "Has Alciel set a trap for us?"

His trepidation was understandable. The central district of Heavensky, one of the most beautiful and well-known spots in all of Efzahan, was eerily quiet.

The reports from the scouts—up until yesterday, anyway—indicated great unrest across the entirety of the capital, as its people anticipated a violent clash between vast human and demon armies. Alciel might have declared martial law across the city in anticipation of this. But the sight before the Phaigan force right now wasn't a city under martial law so much as an abandoned ruin.

Here, in the very center of this vast capital, not a single soul could be found. Along the wide road that led to Heavensky Keep, all that greeted them were the holy-magic lampposts lining the street and the moonlight that occasionally made its way between the clouds. That, and the dark, heavy wind.

"Quite ominous," the lead general muttered as he wiped the sweat from his brow. "I almost feel the breath being taken from me."

"You can follow after me."

The general, surprised, turned toward a mounted figure that had silently approached him.

"L-Lady Emilia?"

"But you may do so only if you are ready to fight. This will be nothing like the towns we've captured before. If you cannot keep up with Olba and me, you will be surrounded by them and you will die."

"..."

As if summoned by her words, Olba guided his own horse behind her. His face was twisted in a frustrated sneer for some reason, the easy self-confidence of the past far gone. Emi flashed him a look.

"I trust you don't mind me leading the advance guard?" she sharply asked.

"...So be it."

The reply came languidly, listlessly, and even to the oblivious general, the mortification in Olba's voice—the realization there was no other reply he could give—was obvious. Emi gave it a satisfied nod and dismounted.

"Sorry I've been so gloomy around you," she said as she caressed her strikingly handsome horse's mane. Then she took a deep breath and raised her voice.

"Manifest yourself, my power, and vanquish those with evil in their hearts!"

A powerful whirlwind, centered around the shouting Emi, made itself known. The torrent of holy force she unleashed—a pillar of light in an otherwise dim evening—was brighter and denser than anything that had so enveloped her in Japan. The Better Half she created from a beam of light in her hand, for that matter, was longer, wider—more of a blunt weapon, almost—than anything that had come before it.

The holy force around her began to take human form, creating a silvery light that surged across her body—the Holy Silver within her, manifesting the Cloth of the Dispeller, the set of armor that could only be described as divine. The round shield borne from her left hand was a new element, one given physical form by Alas Ramus, the Yesod fragment this Hero was bonded with. Emi's long hair turned into silken strands of bluish silver, as if purified by the holy force within her, and her eyes became a brilliant shade of scarlet—a color that had struck fear into many a demon's heart before, and would soon again.

The full and complete form of Emilia Justina, the Hero who saved the entirety of Ente Isla from oblivion, was now here, in a Heaven-sky once again ruled over by demons.

The volunteer forces witnessing this transformation, almost like the creation of a new moon right here on the ground, were so moved by her sheer majesty that, as one, they let out a mighty battle cry. Now they were sure of their upcoming victory. This time, for sure, the Hero of the Holy Sword would lead them against the darkness that threatened to overcome Ente Isla, and they would emerge victorious. There was no longer any doubt in their minds.

Listening to the cheers behind her, Emilia, still enveloped in the light, allowed a self-effacing smile to reach her lips. Some Hero she was. She was in her complete form, far more powerful than even when she confronted Satan in his Devil's Castle, and right now she was nothing more than the opening act.

"Right," she whispered within the torrent, too soft for even the adjacent Olba to hear. "Let's see what kind of theater props Alciel has in mind for this."

Now her smile was fearless, intrepid. It was the broadest one she had made in quite some time, as she soundlessly ascended into the air. She was the very picture of a heavenly warrior, and it earned another hearty cheer from the assembled forces.

"...We're off, Olba."

"Very well, but... I tell you, if you try anything strange here..."

"Oh, I'm perfectly aware of that. I'm putting everything on the table against Alciel. That's what you want, right?"

"...Mmh."

Olba gritted his teeth. But he knew Emilia hadn't given up her wheat fields yet, which offered him some solace as he lifted himself up into the air from the saddle.

"We seek the head of Alciel, the Great Demon General of Heavensky Keep! All of you, follow me!"

"Raaaahhhhh!!"

The excited roar of the volunteer troops echoed across the empty city.

"Don't fall behind, Olba! Heavenly Fleet Feet!"

Like a bolt of moonlight penetrating the darkness, Emilia stormed across the capital streets. Olba flew on behind her, and soon after came the hoofbeats of several thousand Eight Scarves knights affiliated with the Phaigan Volunteer Force.

"Demons to the right!" Emilia sharply pointed out to Olba, not slowing down for a moment. "They're here!!"

"Ngh!!"

Before even bothering to turn in that direction, Olba released a torrent of wind blades toward his right. Hot on their heels was a large horde of Malebranche, and now more than a few of them had fallen down upon the roofs of nearby residences, taken down by the blades. But these were seasoned fighters, and it would take more than that to stop them.

"Run!! Don't worry about their minions!! We seek none but Alciel!!"

Emilia's order made the forces running for the central district push themselves even faster. She gave neither Olba nor the rest of the troops any time to strike lethal blows against the Malebranche. The platoons of demons that flitted around them like flies clearly numbered too few to effectively defend the city, and their formations were set up in such a way that, to Emilia, they were simply lining up to be slain. They must have been aware of this, because their attacks involved either flinging bolts of demonic force from a safe distance, or taking a slash-and-move approach with their swords and claws.

It made little sense to her. There were supposed to be Eight Scarves soldiers in the central district—where were they? If Alciel wanted a full-frontal battle with Emilia and her forces, it was unthinkable that he wouldn't set a single trap along the wide roads to block their forward progress. The Malebranche should be using the forces that remained to defend the city, but all she was seeing here were private-class demons trying their best to hide how outnumbered they were.

But neither Olba nor the rest of the soldiers stopped to ponder this odd state of affairs. Emilia didn't let them; as long as she could keep showing off her dazzling powers, those who followed her would believe that she'd save them in the end, no matter what. She knew that from experience. And Olba, a human and friend of the Hero—more of a sidekick to her, the way she was handling him—was helpless to do anything against her might. Not as long as Emilia was sticking to the script.

So the volunteer force, led by Emilia and rushing down the wholly unblocked streets of the capital at top speed, arrived before the gates of Heavensky Keep in the blink of an eye. Once there, they lined up in front of the keep's large western gate, which was closed. Some of the rear-guard forces were caught in isolated pockets of combat with the Malebranche, but the momentum was still clearly on Emilia's side.

"Right..."

"..."

Keeping a close eye on their surroundings, Emilia and Olba looked up at the keep.

"I am Emilia, the Hero! I ride with the Phaigan Volunteer Force, and we have come here to free the capital of Heavensky! Show yourself, Great Demon General Alciel!"

"Mmm...?"

The force of strength behind Emilia's voice made it hard for Olba to hide his anxiety. All this time, the Hero's attitude toward this campaign could be described as unmotivated at best, outright hostile at worst. But now the will she was showing in the midst of this battle was just as strong as it was during her first fight with the Devil King's Army. Even stronger, in fact.

"...This 'cold tofu'... This 'ginger'... What could it be?"

His pawn's entire attitude had changed the moment she'd read the demon general's letter. Olba had no reason to doubt Emilia's words, but still, the performance worsened his anxiety.

"Ahh! Look at that!!"

Suddenly, shouts of fear began to emanate from the volunteer forces, so emboldened by Emilia's strength a moment ago.

"Could it be...?"

"H-here he comes!!"

"!"

From high above their heads, Emilia could see a figure standing on a Heavensky Keep balcony.

"How nice of you to appear—Emilia the Hero, and the filthy army of human rebels latched on to her!"

The volume of the voice was all it took to overwhelm the volunteers. A voice infused with demonic power, one that seemed to toll the bell of death with every syllable, instantly drained the will among the weaker-minded troops.

The man who now appeared high aloft in Heavensky was not Shirou Ashiya, the Sasazuka resident in the stretched-out shirt and worn-out pants fretting over every little change to his bank account. This was Alciel, the Great Demon General with the authority to direct masses of demon troops, the former conqueror of Ente Isla's Eastern Island. One look was all it took to see that the armor covering his torso and the cape blowing in the wind were all of first-class make—perfectly suited for a Demon General, and only serving to amplify the ominousness and doom that oozed from his every pore.

The glares he exchanged with Emilia across the night sky seemed to make the very air between them twist and warp.

"How truly pathetic of you, Emilia the Hero!" Alciel's voice rang out in its full demonic splendor. "You are aware of the great force behind my 'cold tofu' and 'ginger,' and still you dare to resist me?!"

"Y-you truly mean that?!" Olba shouted in surprise. "What *are* these horrid things?!"

Emilia gauged his reply from the corner of her eye, trying to restrain a laugh. She had to stay strong here. She had to give the signal. The signal that she heard Alciel's message loud and clear.

"*You* are the pathetic worm here, Alciel! Your 'ginger' is as good as useless in the face of the 'cold tofu' of myself, and my holy sword! Wait as long as you like; that will never change in either of our lives!"

"...Hmph. Very well."

Emilia could see the grin on one side of Alciel's face as he stared down at her from high, high above.

"If that's how it shall be, then it is time to muster my forces and make you face cruel reality! Emilia the Hero! Our previous clash may have ended in a draw, but now I challenge you to a one-on-one duel!"

"I accept that challenge!!"

"W-wait, Emilia, that could be... Huh?!"

To an uninformed observer, Olba was hurriedly attempting to keep Emilia from walking into a trap Alciel was undoubtedly ready to set upon her. But Emilia was already ascending into the air—and two figures had come between her and Olba.

"I would hope you are not the kind to interfere in this duel. Your, and my, people's pride are at stake."

"I have things I would like to ask you myself. If you insist in meddling, we will step up to stop you!"

It was Farfarello, the young Malebranche chieftain, and Barbar-iccia, the head warrior who once attempted to lead the entire New Devil King's Army.

"I know not what sort of tricks you and the angels have been up to," a clearly anguished and regretful Barbariccia continued, "but know that Lord Alciel is hardly as foolish as we were. Once this is over, I will gladly accept whatever punishment is handed down to me. But when the ax falls, know that I will be taking you along with me."

"Ngh..."

Olba winced. Even he would face difficulty emerging victorious against two chieftains at once. And even if he pulled off the feat, he would be in no shape afterward to involve himself in Emilia and Alciel's confrontation.

Now he was sure of it: This plan was starting to jump the tracks. Emilia had enough power, he was sure, to vaporize Alciel and these two captains in an instant. That was supposed to be how he and his "friends" wanted this operation to end. Didn't any of them see anything odd about this?

Emilia, meanwhile, paid the panicking Olba no mind. She and Alciel were now higher than the heights of Heavensky Keep itself, facing down each other in the stratosphere. Silver holy light and demonic black light dominated the skies, but otherwise the scene was one of terrifying tranquility.

Alciel spoke first.

"...It has been a while."

"...It has."

"You had just as many Eight Scarves with you the last time you stormed this castle, if I recall."

"And you had a lot more demons."

"I was not lying, you realize. I did not consider that at all a defeat."

"Yeah, yeah, 'strategic withdrawal,' I know."

Then Emi flitted even higher into the air, turning her face in the direction of the heavy stormclouds.

"I remember...the Devil King appeared from the sky back then, too."

The two of them recalled the events of some two years ago. Emilia's forces had freed every district of Heavensky, thus quelling demon rule across the entirety of the Eastern Island. All that stood before the Hero at that point was Alciel. The battle nonetheless extended several hours, before it became clear that Emilia's overwhelming strength gave Alciel no chance to win.

It was at that exact moment when, as Alciel risked his life lunging at Emilia, a voice had rung out behind him. The voice of the one enemy Emilia had wanted to confront more than anyone else—confront, and then kill. The voice of Satan, the Devil King. Even with Alciel and the other Great Demon Generals pinned to the wall, even with most of the world back in human hands, that voice...that figure...that sheer demonic force...filled Emi with a potent mixture of hatred and fear.

The very one who had destroyed everything in her life was before her eyes, and when she first felt the full brunt of his strength, it only served to stir up more hatred within her, more overwhelming terror. If she lost to this force, the world, her father's soul, her home village—it would all end, without any hope of salvation. Even now, she had never forgotten the dark, heavy, painful place her emotions brought her to at that moment.

There, before her eyes, the Devil King had remonstrated Alciel for throwing away his life in an attempt to seize victory from the jaws of defeat. He had come simply to order his general to retreat—and there, he and Emilia exchanged their first words with each other.

The Hero and the enemy of the world.

" "

" "

And for some reason, Emilia—now back to reality—couldn't quite remember what they had each said. But that was just a memory, and absolutely not one she needed to recall right now. She shook her head a little and focused her eyes back on Alciel.

"Is he really coming?"

"I promise you he will. When, exactly…I cannot say. But when he does, certain things may happen."

Alciel knew Maou was coming, but not even he could guess exactly how the demon lord's presence would change things. But even if they didn't go into detail right now, Emilia and Alciel were in agreement on one thing: Whatever he did, Maou would do nothing to destroy the time they had spent together in Japan.

"So if that is clear, we have some business to handle now…"

"Yep. If we can't do anything, we have to keep dancing as long as we're able to. Right?"

"Precisely." Alciel made a fist, stuck his chest out high, and watched as Emilia let the moonlight glint off her holy sword.

"Before we begin," she said, "I probably need to apologize. I was weak, and so I…I killed a lot of your people from the demon realms… I'm sorry."

"It… All it means is that you, and myself for that matter, lacked the power to dominate the scene to our liking. We can clean up once the war is over. More important than that…" Alciel sized up Emilia's sword in its so-called "final form," more majestic than ever before. "I suppose Alas Ramus is healthy?"

"Oh, very. She's a lot stronger than any of us, you know."

"Ah, how it gladdens me to hear!" Alciel exclaimed as he targeted Emilia with a lunging strike, fast enough to leave sound itself in the dust. Without a moment's hesitation, Emilia used the shield on her left arm to block the brunt of it. The shock wave shook the wind itself, creating a clanging noise loud enough to be heard by the throngs of onlookers.

"I was not going easy with that, you realize."

"I told you, Alas Ramus is stronger than us! Hyaaahh!!"

With Alciel's head thrown back by the impact, Emilia stiffened her body and unleashed a kick toward his unguarded chest, the Cloth of the Dispeller turning her legs into lethal weapons. Her foot struck home with a high-pitched thud.

"…Oww!"

The pain surging from her toes almost brought tears to Emilia's eyes. They both fell back, as if the past two strikes were just a pre-arranged practice strike.

"Guess your body's just as stubborn as your head, huh?"

"Indeed. It even sent Durandal flying. If you will not be serious about this, you'll be unable to even scratch me."

"...This is gonna drag on a lot longer than I thought, huh?"

"You need to fight with your full powers from time to time. Your battle senses will start to atrophy otherwise."

"Oh, that's rich, hearing that from you! Don't come crying to me once this is all over!"

Emilia smiled defiantly. Her sword sparkled a bright white as she casually swung it forward.

"Heavenly Storm Fang!!"

"Nnnnngh?!"

A storm of pure light, one that dwarfed what she had used to blow Maou away in Shinjuku, pummeled Alciel's entire body. He tried to steel itself against its vicious force. It left him hopelessly unable to react to Emilia—who, even now, was flying faster than the wind itself at him.

"Air Rush!!"

"Grrhhn!!"

It was a martial-arts move that Albert had taught her, and she unleashed it at whip-fast speed. It landed above Alciel's midsection, sending him flipping through the air. Even the force of the wind it generated was enough to peel off a few roof tiles from Heavensky Keep, despite the holy magic that protected it. She watched them flutter to the ground far below.

Alciel used his demonic force to stop his momentum, but Emilia was already close upon him.

"Heavenly Flame Slash!!"

"Not so fast!!!!"

The Hero's flames, which had singed the Great Demon General Lucifer in Sasazuka once upon a time, were smothered by Alciel's sheer force of will. Her sword was down, and Alciel saw his opening.

He twirled in the air, aiming for the tip of her shoulder, and smashed his leg down against it.

"Enh...!!"

The Cloth might have protected her, but taking a full-power strike from a Great Demon General on her sword-wielding arm made Emilia wince in pain. It also left her wide open.

"Wh-what are...?!"

The next thing she knew, Emilia's entire body was immobilized. Wisps of telekinetic light extended themselves from Alciel's hands, robbing the Hero of her freedom.

"Hohhhhhh..."

"Ah, ah, whoa, hang, hang on a...!!"

The strands of force wrapped themselves around Emilia in a frenzy of undulating activity.

"Ha-ha! Twirl on, my pretties!"

"Wha, whoa, you, you don't have to sound, like, like a villain...!!"

She tried to resist, but now Alciel was in his element. Emilia was bound, unable to move the way she wanted.

"Yaahhhh!"

"You fool!!"

The moment the centrifugal force acting upon him was at its strongest, Alciel spun Emilia straight down to the roof of Heavensky Keep. It would be enough to smash any regular person to bits, with nothing left to identify them, and Emilia took the blow face-first. The physical force of the strike made the roof explode into a million pieces, as if someone had set a series of time bombs on the other side. It resulted in Heavensky Keep, renowned as the most magnificent building in all of Eastern Island, being fully exposed to the elements, like a bald man whose toupee had just flown off.

"...Get up, Emilia! I know you are not fragile enough to give up in the face of this alone!"

"...Yeah. Yeah, I'm not. I know I have to go all in on this. I know, but..."

Emilia, fresh from doing a convincing impression of a meteorite upon the keep, leaped to her feet among the rubble.

"But you hit me right on the bridge of my nose! That *hurt*!"

She held her holy sword with both hands, rubble trailing behind her as she shot like a rocket into the sky, making a beeline toward Alciel.

"Shaahhhhhh!!!!"

"Whoooooaaaah!!"

Like a shooting star of silver, the Better Half carved a beautiful arc into the sky. The path it took was traversed all too quickly, making Emilia look like a mere ball of silver to the crowd below. They could have never imagined that the *ting*s and *clang*s that accompanied every swing indicated that Alciel was predicting, and blocking, every single one of these light-speed strikes.

Alciel boasted the strongest body of the Devil King's Army, but he had not grasped the sort of variety of magical attacks enjoyed by Lucifer and Malacoda. It was his sheer strength that explained why he held sway over so many powerful demon families, why he managed as general to keep the human race from victory for so long to the end. It let him defend against an Alas Ramus–enhanced Better Half in its final form with his bare hands—how could any normal human hurt him?

Simply displaying this force to the elite soldiers of the Eight Scarves was enough to make them fall to their knees in fealty to the Great Demon General. That force was on completely equal footing with Emilia's slashing strikes, and the back-and-forth seemed like it'd continue for some time to come. But:

"Shock wave of Light!!"

"Nh!"

The moment the spell was completed, a light-borne shock wave, not a sword, expanded across Emilia's body. Alciel, focused on dodging another slash, hesitated for a moment—just long enough to feel a glint of warmth on his fingertips. His vision was flooded by the light—the light that had made the Malebranche quiver over the ocean at Choshi—but it made Alciel feel no physical pain at all.

It did, however, provide just enough light to blind Alciel for a moment. And that tenth of a second or two was all Emilia needed.

Soon, her leg was between his arms, still outstretched from deflecting the previous strike.

"Hrahh!"

"Uurrr!"

And then her heel smashed into his chest.

There was no apparent wound on the surface. But the shock wave of the Hero's full-power kick coursed through his body, turning him into yet another meteorite crashing into the keep. The results gouged a large hole into its topmost floor. The more Emilia and Alciel fought, the more Heavensky Keep was battered—roof bits flying, walls falling apart, terraces being crumbled. It wasn't a pretty sight for architecture buffs.

"Back at you, Alciel! Stand up! That's not all you have!"

Now it was Alciel who was slowly peeling himself from the wreckage.

"…Hmph. Do not complain to me if you push yourself too far and run out of gas later."

"I could say exactly the same thing to you!"

"Impudent nonsense," Alciel grumbled to himself as he floated back upward. "But a word of caution. Try not to damage the keep too much. If you raze it down to its foundation, you will regret it later."

"What?"

Alciel gave a carefree smile, like some demonic parent telling his child an important secret.

"Nord Justina is being held in the Cloud Retreat," he said. "He is under guard, but if we continue to wreck this castle and the damage reaches the retreat, there is no telling what might happen. He has made it this far—I would not want you to lose your father for the sake of this charade."

It would be difficult to express Emilia's feelings at that exact moment. A sort of shocked surprise, one that riveted her in place so tightly that she could barely breathe, came first. Then tears welled in her eyes as her cheeks turned a shade of crimson. Part of the dream she had been chasing all this time was now almost within arm's reach.

"…Really?" she gasped.

She had no way of knowing how Alciel had traveled from Japan to Ente Isla. But she now knew that Gabriel had been telling her the truth—that her father was alive in Japan.

"My father…was really there? In Japan? Close to me?"

"I could not say how close, exactly. His Demonic Highness discovered him first."

"…He did?"

It was Maou who had found him? Emilia chewed over the words, evaluating each one before tucking them away in her heart.

"But Nord cannot return to you like this. The power broker running this stage is watching over us in this battle. If you try anything untoward, Nord will be taken someplace where you will never reach him—in an instant."

"…Oh," came the soft reply.

"What is wrong? Lost your will to fight?"

Alciel knew it was pointless to ask the question. The scarlet color of Emilia's eyes told the story: They were eagerly brimming with spirit.

"Thanks. I feel better now."

"You look like you are about to raze the entire world."

"Kind of a rude thing to say to a woman, isn't it? But thanks. I'm ready to keep on dancing now…and to kick up a little dust when the dance is over, too."

"…Perfect!"

Alciel twirled his cape back, his body pulsing in eerie light, and charged once more at Emilia. The holy energy coursed across her body as she readied her blade, bracing herself in midair to swing back.

✳

By the dim light of a candle stand, Sadao Maou was holding his LED lantern and whining to himself.

"Yawwwn… Ooh, dark."

"Yeah, dark. No kidding. How're you feeling?"

He put the lantern down and looked at Acieth, who was sitting up in her bed.

"Mm… The head hurts a little… My neck, too…"

"I'll bet, given that flight you took."

Propelling enough energy out from your forehead to rocket into the sky would be physically trying for anyone. Just thinking about the resulting stress on her neck muscles made Maou's own back ache a bit.

"What happened, I sort remember. But the why…?"

"Like I'd have any idea," Maou replied, dejected. After their splash-down in the lake, he had attempted to carry the unconscious Acieth back to the inn. But, as he should have expected, he was greeted by men from the Inlain Crimson Scarves, tipped off by the tavernkeeper from earlier. They had, to say the least, a few questions for him.

"So…what did you say?"

"I name-dropped Suzuno and the Church. Then I bribed the Inlain Crimson guys to shut them up."

"Oof."

It was, as far as Acieth could figure, the worst possible way Maou could have defused the situation. Nobody was injured, but the two of them had blown a hole in the middle of town, and that was just the start of their ridiculousness. In any normal situation, they should have been sitting in a cell by now. But thanks to Suzuno's Church standing—and the presence of her signature in the inn's ledger—Maou had turned the ruckus into an international incident beyond the hands of a mere Eight Scarves patrolman. He had every reason, however, to expect knights higher up on the food chain to come after him tomorrow, or the next day.

"So, yeah, we're gonna want to be out of this inn ASAP. If you're feeling okay, I wanna get moving."

"Okay…" Acieth meekly watched Maou as he returned to the lantern. Squinting in the dim light, she could see Maou spinning something around in his hands as he held the lantern on its side. "Maou? What are you doing? Making the weird sounds."

"Suzuno and Albert still haven't contacted me. It's been eight hours since they left."

"Eight hours?! That long... Maou!"

"Don't bitch at me for not waking you up, okay? You weren't all that well, either, and as long as we don't know what's going on with you, we can't make any rash moves. That's for your sake as much as mine."

His hand was pointed at Acieth's forehead. She touched it. Even now, it was letting off a faint light. Maou wanted to carp at her about the pains he went through to keep that hidden from the patrolmen, but there was little point to it.

She looked back at him.

"What you are doing? Is that helping contact them?"

"I'm keeping the phone charged, is what I'm doing. I've got no power, so I gotta make sure I'm as receptive to Idea Links as I can be. Ugh, it's a miracle this thing didn't break in the water."

He was turning the crank on his all-in-one LED lantern/radio/phone charger, a handy item to have on an alien planet. The phone was last charged up back when he exchanged digits with Albert, and even with how old and featureless it was, it was still running on empty. Whether it was an issue with his phone model or how he was using the thing, he couldn't say, but as hard as he cranked, he couldn't make the phone charge up as quickly as the instruction manual described. He had been at it for three hours now. Maybe getting immersed in water wasn't so good for the hardware after all.

"I think I'm gonna get tendinitis if I keep this up," Maou said with a wry grin. "These human bodies are so damn weak. Not that it matters now, though..."

He took another look at Acieth's forehead.

"But listen, Acieth, what do you think? You think Alas Ramus is fighting?"

She shook her head. "...I don't know," she whispered. "But before, my chest, it was full of warm feeling. I could not hold it back."

"Yeah, that wasn't all you couldn't hold back there. As I'm sure you remember."

Maou was referring to something else that had been warm and kept inside her. Acieth nimbly ignored the jab.

"But now," she meekly continued as she pointed at a direction in the air, "I know. Over there. The Yesod has lots and lots of power. It is striking a dark, dark force."

"So...southeast of here? Toward the center of the capital?"

Maou attempted to focus his mind on the direction, even though he knew he couldn't sense anything in his current state. But if Acieth was talking about "lots and lots" of power, Emi must have been pushing out the sort of holy force she used against Gabriel once upon a time. If she was, there was no way Maou could miss that, even out here in the medieval exurbs.

But he couldn't detect it.

"Damn it," he muttered, making a fist at nothing in particular. "What is *wrong* with me?"

He knew that stewing in his own juices wouldn't solve anything. And things were only getting worse. Suzuno and Albert were supposed to be in the middle of Heavensky. Where were they? If Alas Ramus was unleashing her full strength, she had to be fighting either Ashiya or an angel. When did that get started? And whether Suzuno had succeeded or failed, shouldn't she have at least called to report back once clashes started breaking out?

"It sucks I can't contact her on my end," he muttered. His lack of demonic force made it impossible to point an Idea Link toward either Suzuno or Albert.

"Hey, Maou? I know right now, it is hard for you. But please! Let's go! My sister, she is near! I can't stand it!"

"..."

Her eyes were pleading. Maou's gaze lingered on her.

In the little while since her stint as a rocket, he hadn't experienced any of the physical illness that had crept up whenever he tried to use her powers. So even if he couldn't harness them, perhaps Acieth could use that strength by herself. She had fought on an even keel with Camael back in Japan; he didn't know how well she'd stack up in Ente Isla, what with all the other types of energy floating around, but at the very least, Acieth wasn't nearly as useless as Maou was right now.

"…Hmm?"

Then Maou's mind recalled the moment he had fused with Acieth.

"Hey, Acieth?"

"What?"

"You were fused with Nord at first, right?"

"Yes?"

"So can you separate from me again?"

"Huh? Ooh, I don't know." Acieth gave him a look of surprise. "I think I could with Pop, but I never tried the returning, so…"

"You haven't? 'Cause you seemed to merge with me pretty easily back at Sasahata North High. You made it sound like moving from Nord to me was a breeze."

"Yes. It was easy, because it was you, Maou. But, you see, I have the issues; perhaps we are not very compatible? And Suzuno and Albert, no way, that will never work."

"Oh?"

"Chiho, ooh, it could work. Amane, maybe, maybe not? Rika or Kisaki, no. Lucifer… We would not get along, no, but I think he is most compatible of all. That evil angel, no way, I don't want to think of, I hope he die. Oh, and the Emi girl, if my sister is okay to her, I think I am, too."

"Um, what?"

This was confusing to Maou. There wasn't any rhyme or reason to who would "work" with her and who wouldn't, from Rika to Emi to the "evil angel" Maou assumed to be Sariel. Maou, Emi, Chiho, Urushihara, and Nord were on the "okay" list; Amane was a toss-up; and Suzuno, Sariel, Albert, Rika, and Kisaki were no good. The fact that Urushihara earned such high marks irked Maou a little. He was afraid to ask how Ashiya and Emeralda ranked.

Then he looked back to their original fusion. He had forgotten about one aspect of it, but now he felt the need to get the facts straight.

"So wait, Acieth, when you say 'latent force,' do you mean…?"

That was what Acieth had called him just before the fusion took place.

"Oh. Yeah. It means can work with me."

Maou appreciated the confirmation. But it led to another question.

"Isn't that weird, though?"

"What is?"

"You're fusing with us, right? Kind of like grafting a new branch onto a tree? So why are we the 'latent' forces to you?"

"Um?" Acieth gave him a blank stare. "It is not so weird, no?"

"Oh?"

"Everyone in this world with intelligence, they are all latent forces of Sephirot. Maou, you have the order upside down, I think."

"The order?"

This only confused Maou further. Acieth didn't give him time to ponder over it.

"Come on, Maou! It doesn't matter! My sister, she in the danger! Take me to her! If you not move, I not move, either!"

"Uh, yeah…"

"If we go, I think maybe, uh, perhaps, me and my sister, we go together and beat up all enemy! You can sit somewhere safe and watch. So please! Let's go! Now!"

"Oof. Now I really don't wanna go."

The poor evaluation of his abilities rankled Maou, but if Alas Ramus was fighting, Emi had clearly kicked something off. He couldn't know with who, exactly, but as mocking as Acieth could be at times, she had never lied to him.

"Acieth."

"What?!"

"Is Emi doing okay? Um, I mean, is Alas Ramus?"

"Ooh, swell! To the moon!"

The reply, if a bit abstract, helped reassure Maou a bit.

"Acieth, do you think you can drive a scooter?"

"Maou! You want to use the scooter?! I think so, yes, but too slow…"

"No. We'll use the scooters as long as Alas Ramus is okay. That's final."

He had a hunch Acieth intended to fly over, like she did when she'd taken Maou from the driver license center in Fuchu to Chiho's high school. He didn't want that to happen.

"Suzuno's an open question, but we know Emi and Alas Ramus are okay. As long as we know that, flying can only hurt us. We have to do everything we can to keep Gabriel and Camael from spotting us. If they find us, they'll take a Gate right over here, and I dunno if we'll get the chance to reach Alas Ramus then. You wanna be sure you can see your sister, right? So chill out. If you start panicking, you'll mess up things you'd be able to pull off otherwise."

"Oh... Okay. I watched you do the riding. And I helped Pop earn his license, too. Or try to. So I try! It will come fast, I'm sure."

"...Yeah."

He didn't like her chances. That, and ugh, that stupid test. He needed to get back at her for that.

"Once we get Emi back, I'm definitely gonna make her pay for that test I had to blow off."

He nodded and gave Acieth a pat on the head.

"Let's get packed up. Hey, Suzuno left the scooter keys in here, didn't she?"

"Maou, can we eat before we go?"

Maou laughed, a little relieved to see Acieth back to normal. "After all that crap you put me through, you want to eat again? Crazy! I want to pick up a few things before we hit Heavensky. We'll eat at the next town over, so just hang on 'til then!"

Acieth gave an understanding smile in response. Then something caught her eye.

"Maou, what about...?"

It was the present Maou had bought for Chiho and Emi just before their rocket trip—a set of three wooden spoons. They were carved from the same tree by a master woodworker, and apparently they brought good luck to the receiver. Chiho's was decorated with a flowery design, almost like cherry blossoms, while Emi's and Alas Ramus's were adorned with a pair of small birds. He had them wrapped up, but their little dip in the lake completely wrecked the box, so he was carrying them out in the open.

"Oh, that? Hmm. Better find some cushioning for these. Don't want to ruin the finish."

Maou looked around the room for something to package them in. Nothing immediately obvious was in sight.

"And luggage of Suzuno and Albert, what about that?"

"Yeah, better bring it along. I doubt we'll be coming back. Takes up a lot of space, though… Maybe we could keep it here and have Albert fetch it later? Ooh, but they might confiscate it after everything we did…"

"Um, Maou? The innkeeper, he said something about the water if we check out?"

"Oh, yeah, the well usage fee and the water for the stables… Man, it sucks having to pay for water. It tasted all weird, too."

With his upcoming departure came a litany of problems. They knew they had to go, but Maou knew he couldn't just leave all their possessions in the room. By the time he had them all packed and picked up his scooters from their hiding place in the stables, another thirty minutes had passed.

THE DEVIL AND THE HERO WITNESS ENTE ISLA'S TRANSFORMATION

"Hey, so was that guy always that strong, or...?"

Raguel, decked out in his usual Afro and punk-chic outfit, eyed Emilia and Alciel duking it out from a high hill on the outskirts of Heavensky. What he saw surprised him.

"I think I remember seeing you kick his ass over in Tokyo Tower, Gabe..."

"Aww, that's just because it was in Japan," Gabriel lethargically replied. "The demonic force he had back there wasn't anything like he can tap over here, you know? That was all cobbled together by you-know-who when she wasn't busy feeding it to Chiho Sasaki."

"You don't think Emilia is going easy on him?"

"Hmm?" Gabriel turned toward another voice, belonging to a large man in red armor accompanied by a small boy.

"The combined powers of Emilia and the Yesod were enough to topple you, were they not, Gabriel? If she is fighting on an even keel with a demon of such a level, what could that possibly mean?"

"Ooh, you don't have to scowl at me like that, Camael. *Someone's* still a little testy about earlier, huh?"

"You have demonstrated a severe lack of follow-through in the past," Camael said, the frustration clear in his voice. "I worry that you are considering this mission complete before its time."

"Wow, talk about trust issues," Gabriel deadpanned, sizing up the expressionless man in the armor. Camael responded by looking down at Erone, the boy next to him.

"Imperfect as she may be, Emilia is the 'latent force' of a Sephirah child. You know as well as I do that such power cannot be treated lightly."

"Ooh, you'd know all about what kinda power that is, huh? 'Specially given how thoroughly Satan whipped you a bit ago."

"...*You*..."

Camael glared at the unflappably flippant Gabriel, even though he knew it would do nothing to stop him.

"...Well, either way, there's no chance in hell that Emilia's gonna lose," Gabriel went on. "And if it looks like she will, maybe it's a bit early, but we can always zoom in and help out, right? I'm not blind, y'know. We'll make contact with her once Alciel and the Malebranche tire her out enough. That's the plan, right?"

"Yeah," Raguel said with a sigh, "but d'you think that's gonna happen anytime soon? How long have they been at it, anyway?"

"A little over ten hours," Camael balefully replied.

That was, indeed, how much time had passed since the battle began. For a duel—even one between two such powerful warriors—it was taking a remarkably long time, and it was happening nonstop and at full force.

"Well, what's the big deal, guys? Just let 'er do what she wants. I know you wanna move things along a little more, but if you panic and botch the landing, you'll wind up wasting your life, mm-kay? Like Sariel did."

"Ah."

"...Hmph."

Raguel and Camael both frowned in unison, a reaction Gabriel couldn't help but smile at.

"So let's just watch 'n' wait, guys. One of 'em should tire out before..."

"!!"

Suddenly, Erone, by Camael's side, sharply shook his head.

"What's up?" the still-smiling Gabriel asked, picking up on it first.

"...Mph."

"What is it?"

Camael and Raguel both looked at Erone. He simply kept looking, far off to the south.

"Something is coming."

As Camael and Raguel continued to give the child puzzled looks, Gabriel turned toward Heavensky. He subtly smiled, something the other two angels couldn't pick up on.

"What's coming, Erone, hmm?"

"Are those..." Erone opened his eyes wide. "...scooters?"

""Scooter?""

"Scooter... Scooter... What was that again? I think I've heard that word before..."

Raguel titled his head and squinted, as Camael searched Erone's face for an answer.

"Well, it's about time..."

Only Gabriel seemed in control of the situation, now smiling broadly as he gauged the sight of Heavensky before him.

✳

On the well-maintained roads of the capital's central district, two scooters sailed along at top speed, engines whining. Sadao Maou, in control of his Honta Gyro-Roof, dolefully eyed Heavensky in front of him, currently illuminated by streaks of silver and black darting to and fro above it.

"What the hell are Suzuno and Albert doing? This is, like, the worst-case scenario, isn't it?!"

"Maou! There! Over there! Sister!!"

Acieth's agitated voice rang in his ears, thanks to the two-way motorcycle radio he thought to invest in.

"Yeah, I know! Calm down! Your language skills go to pot when you're too excited!"

"Maou! This is enough! I want to fly! The angels, they don't matter anymore!"

"I told you, chill out! Heavensky's huge! We're not as close to the center as it looks! We're too far away to get support from her if we need it... Whoa, here it comes!"

They had arrived at one of the large gates that opened into the nobles' quarter of the city. It was manned by a large number of knights, and Maou could tell the sight of two scooters from Japan trundling up was unnerving them greatly. It was probably the rear guard from the Phaigan Volunteer Force, and now—with blasts of holy magic and rains of arrows—they were gunning for their rides.

"*Maou! What now?!*"

"Full speed ahead! I ain't scared of no holy magic!"

"*What?! Scared or no, if it hits you, you hurt!*"

"I'm fine! Just trust Japanese engineering a little, all right? Ahhhhh!!"

He revved up the engine again and hurtled himself straight into the storm of fire from the force in front of them. "*Agh, here goes nothing!*" Acieth shouted from behind.

Arrows and magic bolts pelted the unique full-sized windshield on Maou's Gyro-Roof. The fiber-reinforced plastic roofs on both of them became dented, warped, pockmarked, and partially melted, but miraculously, they still managed to keep the drivers safe.

"*Ooh, wow!*"

"Boo-yah! Don't let anyone tell you that 'made in Japan' don't mean anything!"

And with a shout and another whine from their engines, the two of them were through the guards. The sheer force and noise they generated made the Eight Scarves men instinctively dive for cover, opening the road for them—and any arrows they shot from behind weren't fast enough to catch up with a Gyro-Roof at full speed.

To the two of them, though, nothing mattered apart from what happened to the two fighters pitting their titanic strength against each other above them.

"Alas Ramus! Ashiya! Emi! I'm heeeeeeere!!"

They were still far off, but now Maou could clearly see Ashiya in demon form up above, trading blows with Emi in half-angel form as she wielded a larger version of her holy sword.

"Maou! Something behind us!!"

He glanced at a side mirror. A platoon of the Eight Scarves knights he had just buzzed was now hot on his heels, their horses going at a full gallop. Some of them already had their bows drawn.

"Chill out, Acieth! Use it now!!"

"What? But it is only bluff! Will it work?!"

"We aren't fighting the Eight Scarves! All we need to do is spook their horses and stop them! Do it!"

"Okeydokey!"

From a pocket on her overalls, Acieth took out a thick, red object—a sheaf of evil-dispelling fireworks from the village she had rocketed out of.

"Good thing I have lighter... Hyaaaaahh!!"

Acieth's scream of joy as she set off the fireworks with her kitchen lighter pounded against Maou's eardrums—but not half as much as the ensuing explosions that surrounded them. The packet of fireworks, held together by a common fuse, erupted in a serious of explosions.

"You idiot! What're you doing?! Throw it! You're gonna burn yourself!"

*"Hyaaahhhh-*koff koff!!!!*"*

The coughing, smoke-blinded Acieth tossed the fireworks to the ground behind her. Maou followed it up by taking out a set of fireworks from his own hoodie, lighting it, and throwing it backward. Loud pops and thick smoke filled the air, and for just a moment, he could see horses rearing up in fright on his side mirror. He sped up.

"Acieth! You okay?"

*"Smoky...*koff!!*"*

"Okay, great! Whoa, look out, there's more of 'em up ahead! Honk your horn!"

"Raaahhhh!!"

Another volunteer force platoon was on patrol around the intersection of two wide roads in the middle of the central district. Their reaction to Maou and Acieth was just as confused, and just as hostile, as the one before.

Soon, though, they were stopped in their tracks by an earsplitting whine—the sound of Maou and Acieth both leaning heavily on their scooters' horn buttons. It was an unfamiliar, offensive sound, and not only did it stun the entire platoon, but the moment they looked toward the source of the noise, they wound up gazing straight into the high beams of their LED headlights. The resulting moment of blindness let Maou zoom past them, leaving another packet of exploding fireworks as a parting gift.

But they had no time to rest. From another street, a cavalry corps had joined the scene to investigate the furor. It had now nearly caught up with Acieth.

"Maou! They have the spears! Come from side!"

"All right! You got any fireworks?"

"I used them! The rest are in scooter box!"

"Why'd you use so many at once?! …Hngh!"

Maou heaved another packet at two mounted soldiers in front of him. Once they were out of the picture, he tossed something else at Acieth.

"Grab it!!"

"What is it?!"

"Spray it into their snouts!!"

"Huhh? Whooaahh!!"

Acieth studied the rather large bottle of outdoor insect repellent Maou just handed her. It was the one piece of camping gear that Suzuno and Maou didn't argue about before purchasing, and the off-label usage he'd just suggested to her was as effective as it was painful. The pungent odor, along with the sensation of being sprayed in the face, made the horses stumble and fall over.

After she looked through her side mirrors to check that none of the fallen cavalrymen were dead, Acieth let off a low grown.

"We very mean to horses…"

"Yeah, well, that's what they get for using 'em in war," Maou said. "I think the coast is clear now. Get some more fireworks out of your box."

He stopped his Gyro-Roof and opened the rear compartment. It had a small mountain of fireworks inside, along with other travel accessories and Suzuno's and Albert's personal belongings. For their current invasion of Heavensky, they had thrown out all the food and water they had brought along—they needed the room for more anti-personnel weaponry.

This "weaponry," of course, was pieced together from whatever they could find in the villages around the agricultural district. It wouldn't be good for anything apart from bluffing. But as Maou saw it, if he actually killed anyone on this operation, it'd leave a bad aftertaste, whether his friends were involved or not. That was the watchword for Maou as he selected his arsenal.

"Hey, Acieth, make sure you can reach your wooden sword at any time, just in case."

"Huh? But I need my arm!"

"You can throw it if you have to. Just try your best not to hurt anyone."

"But why? It is fine, no? I am not sure way of fighting is good…"

Acieth had a point. They were riding around without helmets, dragging wooden swords behind them, throwing firecrackers all over the place, honking their horns constantly, and blinding people with their high beams. The King of All Demons and the miraculous child of a Sephirah seed were essentially a biker gang. Though, really, most biker gangs in Japan weren't the kind to be as much of a public nuisance as these guys were. It was almost a shame they hadn't equipped their scooters with exhaust whistle tips and horns that played the national anthem.

"We're just getting started, man!" Maou exclaimed. "The closer we get to the keep, the harder it'll be to shake 'em off. That's what this is for."

The next thing out of his scooter's compartment was a corked bottle that contained some sort of viscous liquid and had firecrackers wrapped around it. A piece of paper, kept in place by the cork, served as a fuse. As an improvised Molotov cocktail, it was a commendable piece of work.

"Are you serious?" Acieth wearily said.

"Yeah!" Maou countered. "At least until we regroup with those two guys up there and Suzuno, wherever the hell she is! If it gets to the point where *you* have to start fightin', I'm probably screwed, so I really wanna save that for when we absolutely need it. Your powers make too much of a racket, y'know?"

"...Oh."

Maou's decision, after they just had their little reckless-driving and vehicular-assault parade, was less than convincing to Acieth's ears. But it didn't matter. Maou liked the classical biker-gang style, and he was sticking to it.

"Suzuno...come back and stop Maou... This, it is awful..."

She listlessly muttered to herself as she relunctantly stuffed fireworks into her pockets.

✳

"...?"

As she deflected what had to be the eight thousandth claw slash from Alciel, Emilia heard an odd sound. A high-pitched whine that was coming closer. Alciel, picking up on it, too, stopped attacking and looked down. It was a very familiar sound to them—but one they'd normally never hear on this world.

"Is that..."

There were two of them, running along at breakneck speeds in front of the volunteer force men chasing them.

""...a pair of pizza delivery scooters?!"" Emilia and Alciel both shouted.

That it was. It was a pair of roofed scooters, often used by pizza shops to bring the goods to customers in Japan.

"Could...could that be...?"

The battle with Alciel, with no apparent end in sight, was starting to fatigue Emilia. She was clinging to hope that the Devil King would appear sometime, but there were moments when she had doubted it'd ever happen, that it was all wishful thinking on Alciel's part. If he was coming, she would've picked up on the presumably massive amount of dark power he'd be wielding, but she had sniffed out nothing. If Maou was showing up, she had no idea how he'd make it here.

"How…how ridiculous can you get…?"

Did he manage to get that license? And for that matter, why was he crashing the Hero and Great Demon General's to-the-death confrontation with that, of all things?

There were two scooters hurtling forward down there, the other one likely manned by either Suzuno or Urushihara. Emilia could tell they were headed straight for the keep. It made her want to smile, but her face quickly stiffened.

"Wh-what's that…?"

The volunteer force men below them had noticed the scooters. It sent them into a frenzy, and already she could see many of them ready their attacks. Yet the two scooters plowed on, never braking or flinching. As they should. If they slowed down, they would be overwhelmed.

"L-look…"

Alciel floated agape in the air. He had forgotten all about attacking, once he realized the truth.

The pair of scooters was leading what must have been the entirety of the royal force straight into the keep.

"Heyyyy!! Come on! I want give up already!! Let me use power!"

Amid the earth and air-trembling rumble, Maou could hear the half-sobbing voice of Acieth through his headset. He couldn't do much for her at the moment.

"Just shut up and throw some firecrackers!"

"They not work anymore!" she countered. *"They know them now! And your bomb, super no good, Maou!"*

"We've made it this far! No turning back now! If we stop here, those hordes are gonna run right over us and our scooters! If you don't feel like getting turned into ground Acieth and scooter parts, keep going!!"

To his side, Maou could see Acieth looking behind her, eyes welling up from the intense wind. His own side mirrors told the whole story—a literal horde. He gritted his teeth.

"*I tell you, I fly, it will be okay!*"

"If we fly outta here, they're gonna trash our scooters! Suzuno'll beat the crap out of me once she finds out! Plus, I'm totally keeping Mobile Dullahan III once I get back! I'm not gonna let these freaks smash it up!"

"*Maou! Who cares?!*"

They were now going at breakneck speed, shooting across the broad path that led straight to the keep, a motley rabble of knights, horsemen, and random hangers-on behind them. The volunteer force troops at the forefront, undaunted by Maou's delinquent biker behavior, were now leading the Eight Scarves cavalry and infantry who didn't join the volunteers, as well as more than a few Malebranche warriors, united against a common enemy. As a royal force, it was lacking any coherent leadership, and now they were almost at the massive gate that circled the keep.

"*Maou! Ahead! Bald man and demons!!*"

Olba, Farfarello, and Barbariccia were already enjoying a front-row view of the battle between Emilia and Alciel by the time Maou crashed into the scene. But there was no braking now—the wolves behind them wouldn't slow down. They'd wind up like a lone jackrabbit against a thundering horde of bison, stampeding across the prairie.

"They don't matter! Full speed ahead! We're plowing right into the castle!!"

"*Oh, no waaaaaay!!*"

Ignoring Acieth's protests, Maou pushed the throttle even harder, letting off a particularly large chunk of firecrackers as a sort of grand finale. The horn button was now permanently activated, thanks to a bit of waterproof camping tape, and his LED lantern (which he wasn't expecting to use any longer) had its emergency siren activated as he lobbed it directly at the volunteer force men awaiting him up ahead.

It was then that Olba, Farfarello, and Barbariccia finally noticed who was leading this ragtag royal army.

"S-Satan? The Devil King?!"

"My liege?!"

"What?! His Demonic Highness?!"

"Yo, guys! I'm kinda busy, so laaaaaterrrrr!!"

He careened past them all, giving himself barely enough time to recognize their faces. The two scooters went right under Olba, who was floating several feet in the air. The resulting gust made his robes flap upward in the wind, exposing the undergarments of the great Church betrayer for all of the grand capital of Efzahan to see.

"Man, I did *not* like what I saw just now, but whatever! Acieth! Keep your speed up! I'm gonna open up your storage box and throw everything out of it!"

"I give up! Whatever you saaaaaaay!!"

Taking position a little behind Acieth, Maou used the edge of his wooden sword to undo the pre-loosened latch on the box and jab at the handle. In a moment, the lid was open. It contained a stash of Maou's handmade Molotov cocktails—and thanks to the gasoline he'd saved after Albert's arrival, he had a ton to work with. In a moment, they shattered against the ground, sending plumes of fuel onto the street.

Then he lit a firecracker and tossed it behind him.

"Hyaaaaaaaaaaahhhhhhh?!"

"Whoa! Ow, ow, ow, ow! Geez, it actually lit that?!"

Maou seemed honestly surprised as the gasoline erupted in a smoky explosion behind him. The wave of heat seared Maou, as well as ignited the firecrackers both he and Acieth had in their hands.

"Ow! Owwww! Hot, hot, hot, hot!"

The blast had quite literally lit a fire under the scooters, but they pressed on past the smoke, the flames, and the general chaos. The light show pushed them past Olba's main volunteer force guard, through the main gate, and safely into Heavensky Keep grounds.

For just a moment, it was too much for Olba and his two demon companions to comprehend. And that moment was all it took. The volunteers pursuing Maou surged through the gate, as if being pulled inside, and all Olba's own men could do was stand there blankly and watch. Now the focus wasn't on Emilia, or Alciel, or Olba and his Malebranche cohorts at all. It was all on Maou, Acieth, and the horde of royal forces as they made a mad rush for the main keep.

The grounds of Heavensky Keep were fairly extensive—large enough to hold both the Cloud Retreat and the keep itself, as well as some imperial gardens and other administrative buildings. But thanks to all the loud explosions and white smoke, it was clear as day where the two scooters leading this mob were.

""Oh.""

Their voices were devoid of energy—chiefly because the white smoke had stopped right in front of the Cloud Retreat's gate.

They could see the vanguard cavalry fall off the drawbridge as they tried to pursue the scooters, or simply smash against the gate's walls, unable to change formation in time. The foot soldiers behind them, still running at full momentum, were soon falling like dominoes as the traffic jam unfolded.

It was a sorry scene, but not one that stopped the scooters' onrush. Soon, white exhaust began to leak out from Cloud Retreat windows, here and there. The whine of two engines could be heard, along with things being smashed up or tossed aside, explosions of unknown causes, people and horses braying in dismay, and all manner of other sounds that formed an everlasting din. You didn't have to be inside the retreat to know that pandemonium was unfolding in there.

Everyone had forgotten about Emilia and Alciel's battle, Emilia and Alciel included. All eyes were focused on the Cloud Retreat, and the biker gang and crazed forces currently laying waste to it. It gave Emilia a chance to notice a slightly brighter sky to the east. Sunrise was coming.

"…Ah! Oh, no!" a flustered Alciel exclaimed. "The Cloud Retreat… We must do something or…"

But in another moment, Alciel's concerns were all in the past.

The heavens shook, then fell apart.

"!"

"Wha…?!!"

Emilia and Alciel opened their eyes wide in shock.

The Cloud Retreat, almost equal in majesty to the Heavensky Keep that Efzahan's emperor ruled the Eastern Island from, was pierced by a dagger of purple light.

In a moment, it began to crumble. The pillar of light cut through the dark clouds above, and there, for all to see, was a red moon and a blue one, ruling over the night.

Emilia looked up. Someone was there—just as he had been before. The Devil King Satan, the despot who fled to Earth before she could land that one final blow, was in the air above the broken Heavensky Keep, surveying the landscape with the two moons behind him.

But not everything was the same as it was on that fateful day. Satan was the Devil King still, yet not the Devil King of yore. The over-whelming demonic force was vintage Satan, through and through. But his exterior was still Sadao Maou, tireless fast-food jockey from Sasazuka.

The Devil King leisurely floated down to Emilia and Alciel, enjoy-ing the eyes of everyone in the city upon him.

"…My liege!"

Alciel fell to his knees, overcome with emotion as he greeted his leader once more.

Emilia simply stood there, frozen. Sadao Maou was right there— the same Maou who kept giving her lip on Earth, who pretended to be what he wasn't, who worked hard every day of his life, who was beloved by the humans around him—who loved the humans back. The most incomprehensible personification of evil in existence.

Then, as if angling for this exact moment, the eastern mountain ridge on the horizon let pass the first arrows of daylight, as strong as the purple streak that still extended from the keep. The dark night took its leave, as if celebrating the advent of its king—and the sun quickly vanquished it for good, welcoming the master of all demons to its domain.

And watching all this unfold, Emilia couldn't help but think: Why couldn't she detect such a massive amount of demonic force until right now? A pity that Sadao Maou—while the quintessential "nice guy"—wasn't nice enough to tell her.

"Ugh, I swear," he said, his voice just as whiny and sullen as usual. "I screw up my license, I owe Suzuno a crapload of money, I take an entire week off work, so I'm in a major cash crunch, I'm gonna have to cover, like, six people's shifts to repay the favor... When it rains, it pours, huh?"

There was nothing at all demonic about his words—and perhaps why they sounded so comforting to Emilia.

"Once we're back, I'm gonna have a word with all of you guys, got it? Also, for all of next month, I don't wanna hear any bitchin' about what I decide to do, and I don't care what you think about it. I don't care how many times it takes; I'm gonna get that damn license. And I'm gonna have my own scooter, too!"

"...As you wish, my liege." Alciel, still kneeling, hung his head low. Then:

"...I'm sorry to put all this on you."

Emilia simply blurted it out. It was far easier for her than she expected. But:

"What? Dude, Emi, what were they feedin' you in your prison cell?"

Maou winced at the sight of a fully dejected Emilia, holy sword still in hand.

"Wh-what is it?"

"Nobody's controlling you or anything, yeah? You're acting so obedient. It's freaking me out."

"..."

Emilia fell silent. Normally this would be where she'd blow her top, but she just couldn't summon the energy.

"Even I'm like that sometimes," she plainly replied, admitting the truth. "I'm not expecting you to forgive me...but if we can all make it back to Japan, I've got something I really need to apologize for."

"Oh...kay? Uh, Ashiya, is something up with Emi, or...?"

Maou, holding enough demonic force to make all of Ente Isla prostrate themselves before his mighty figure, looked honestly spooked as he sized Emilia up.

"Perhaps, Your Demonic Highness. But...during this unplanned excursion into Ente Isla, I believe both Emilia and myself have experienced a great deal of things. I would advise you to save your judgment of her sanity for after we return to safe harbor and discuss matters in depth. Both she and I have expended a great deal in the previous battle."

"...All right."

The explanation grabbed Maou's attention. He raised his head, looked down upon the half-ruined Cloud Retreat, and spoke.

"Hey! Get up here!"

Emilia and Alciel turned toward where he faced. From the thin bar of light, they could see something slowly emerge. The glare from the mix of purple and sunlight made it hard to discern the figure's face, but the moment she spotted the large man being held from his back, Emilia's heart almost exploded in her chest.

"Emi, I'm not expecting you to forgive me for everything. Not at this point. But maybe I can make up for it a little by giving you back something I found—something important to you. 'Course, I just kinda stumbled upon him—I didn't, like, do anything for him. And he just happened to be in there, so I figured, hey."

"...Ah," came the voice directly from Emilia's soul.

He must have been a decent amount older from when she'd last seen him. But the stout body, the relaxed expression... There was no way she couldn't recognize him. No way she could forget him. In an instant, her holy sword disappeared into thin air, and her open arms embraced the body as it was presented to her by the smaller figure below. She could feel his body heat, his pulse—and Emilia's own pulse quickened.

He felt so light to her. The Emilia Justina of today was sturdy (and holy magic–infused) enough that being slammed against a castle roof by a Great Demon General bothered her as much as getting flicked on the tip of her nose. She was no longer a clueless young girl who cried over every little thing; but now she didn't bother holding the tears back.

Hearing it in words didn't make it feel real to her. It didn't, and that was why she found it so difficult to reach an answer. But now that the conclusion was in her arms, Emilia knew. She wasn't any sort of Hero at all.

"Fa...ther..."

The man, his breathing shallow but relaxed as he slept, was in the prime of his life, his face now visible in the purple light. Her father—the man she never thought she'd see again—was alive and and in her embrace. That alone made Emilia feel truly fulfilled inside, as if all the battles in her life were over.

She was no bastion of light, fighting for all that was Good and Just. She was Emilia, the farmer's daughter who simply wanted her father back.

"I...I'm not dreaming..."

She felt her heart slow down, as if the chains of self-loathing binding it tight had been released.

"No, you sure ain't. So could you put up a barrier for him already, man? And, Ashiya, can you maybe give the guy a little breathing space?"

"Uh..."

"Hmm? Oh. Yes, my liege."

"Oh, um, ummm, right. Oof!"

Alciel, his body still exuding the kind of demonic force that would kill most humans, took a step back. Emilia, snapping out of her daze, wiped her eyes as she enveloped her father, Nord, in a barrier of holy magic.

"But that's not everything yet. Is Alas Ramus all right?"

"...Of course," Emilia said, still wiping the tears. "She was bursting with energy when we were fighting Alciel, and... Hmm? What was that?"

She blinked at the sudden outburst from the child in her mind.

"Wh-what? All right, all right. Hooph!"

The frantic urging made Emilia summon her—this time as Alas Ramus, not as her sword. The child of Yesod promptly turned an eye to the relatively small figure underneath Nord's body.

"Daddy!"

"Yo, Alas Ramus."

The sight of his daughter in good spirits made Maou's face soften.

"I brought someone here I think you'll probably wanna say hello to."

"...Okay," she said with a nod, already knowing who it was. Soon, they were at each other's side.

"Hi, A-ceth!"

At that moment, the tower of light spouting from the Cloud Retreat faded into thin air. Their faces were now illuminated by the rapidly advancing dawn.

"My...sister..."

The sight made both Emilia and Alciel gasp a little. Acieth was clearly more mature, but from the silvery forelocks to the single shock of purple, she was a dead ringer for Alas Ramus.

"D-Devil King?! Wh-who's this girl?!"

"My liege, could that be another...?"

"A-ceth..."

"Ooh, boy, long time no see, huh, sis?"

The two spawn of Sephirah gauged each other—one looking straight ahead, the other turned downward in shame.

"Yeh!"

"I very surprised. Sis, you are still baby!"

"A-ceth so big!" Alas Ramus exclaimed with a smile.

"...Yeah," her sister replied, feeling even more self-conscious.

"A-ceth?"

"...Hnnh...!!"

Then Acieth, face still turned down, began to quiver. As they all watched, her face twisted in pain. Then it became overridden with tears.

"Ahhhh!! My sister!! I wanted see you so baaaaaaadddddd!!"

The brave facade crumbled all too easily as Acieth's eyes and nose began to free-flow, her arms tightly clutching Alas Ramus. She sobbed freely, Alas Ramus appreciating the emotion if not all the gunk on her face.

"Eww! A-ceth all messy!" she said with a sniff. But she didn't push her away.

"My siiiiisssterrrrrrr!!!! Waaahhhhh!!!!"

"A-ceth, don't cry! Be a good girl!"

It appeared that Alas Ramus really did play the big-sister role in the family. After all the crying she did at all the mean stuff grown-ups made her do—from wearing dirty diapers to performing the bidding of archangels—there she was, patting her younger sister's hair, the solid rock to Acieth's torrential snot-flood.

"Bwwaaaahhhhhh!!!! I so looooonnnely!!!! Siiiiisssss!!"

"Uh, Devil King?"

"My liege, what are we witnessing...?"

Maou grinned at them both. "Guess that's two tearful reunions in one day, huh?"

"Uh...yeah..."

"If you say so, my liege," a confused Alciel replied. He and Emilia gauged each other for a moment. They had fought to the death for ten hours straight until a few moments ago, but all that tension was gone now, mere dust in the wind. Now they were back to playing the rules of Shirou Ashiya and Emi Yusa, befuddled and unnerved by the erratic behavior of the demon lord reigning from a one-room Sasazuka apartment.

"One thing's for sure: We're definitely gonna need to sit down and have one hell of a family discussion when we get home."

"Uh...yeah..."

"If you say so, my liege..."

"Guys, you're looping on me... Oop."

Before he could continue, Maou was interrupted by something that

couldn't have been more out of place in this scene—an ever-so-tiny ringtone. Emilia and Alciel looked around, searching for the source, but their question was answered when Maou fished something out of a pants pocket.

"That's yours?" Emilia said as she recognized the battered, beaten phone in his hand. It was an old flip type, with the outer side half-melted and the hinge broken, leaving the inner wiring open to the elements. Maou managed to pry it open, revealing a screen just as shattered as everyone expected. But it still took calls. A little corner of the LCD was still lit, and the half-exposed vibration circuit was making the entire phone shake dangerously.

"Nice, huh?" Maou said, grinning as he showed it to Emilia. "I kinda burned it, shot firecrackers at it, dropped it in a pond... It sort of cracked up when I crashed the scooter in there, too. But how d'you like that? All this screen and shell damage, and all the internal components are just fine. No way your smartphone can do this! Good thing I remembered to charge it."

He was still grinning as he pushed the Accept button. Even with the screen bashed in, he found out who was calling pretty fast.

"What are you doing, you imbecilic Devil King?!!!!"

The loud griping through the incoming Idea Link battered Maou's eardrum. It was imposing enough even for Alas Ramus and Acieth to hear.

"Geez, pipe down. You guys were out screwin' around for so long, Acieth lost her patience."

Alas Ramus's eyes sparkled. "Ooh, Suzu-Sis?"

"Do you think we have had it easy, you buffoon? What did you do?! Why is there a massive scrum of fallen volunteer forces in front of the Cloud Retreat?!"

"Oh, can you see the keep from where you're at? Well, don't worry, okay? I got the scooters into just a little bit of a fender-bender, but it'll be super easy to fix—"

"Answer me! Is your power back?! Oh, by all that is holy, did you total the scooters?! Have you no respect for the personal property of others, Mao—"

"Hey, Acieth, here."

"Huh? Ah? Oh? Ummm, hello? Suzuno?"

"Acieth?! Acieth, is that you?!"

"Yeah, um, umm…"

Acieth wiped her still-reddened face with her free hand. Then she stuck out her tongue.

"Um, I felt my sister close to me, and I, uh… Ooh, excited. *Very* excited."

"~~~~~~~~~~~~~~~~~~~~~~!!"

"Suzuno? Suzuno, I not understand you! …Oh, you want Maou? Okay!"

"Yeah, so there's the story, I guess."

"You guess?!! Devil King, what have you done?!"

"Eesh, what's the big deal?"

Maou looked down. Next to Heavensky Keep lay the Cloud Retreat. It had taken extensive damage from the keep's rubble in addition to Maou's rampage, to the point that he could hardly recognize its original structure.

"Emilia's father and the Azure Emperor are in there!!"

"Yeah, I know."

"…Hahhhh?!"

He could almost feel Suzuno's spittle hitting his ear through the Idea Link.

"Acieth swapped me out for Nord in there, and I got my demon force back thanks to that."

"W-wait! So, so Emilia has seen her father?! But what of the emperor?!"

"Oh, that old coot? He's cool. Libicocco'll bring him over there later. I guess Ashiya had it all arranged that way in advance. So I heard you guys snuck in here or something?"

"What? Alciel?! This is making no sense to me!"

It wouldn't make sense to anyone.

Maou hadn't spoken enough with him yet to know the whole story, but he already had a sense of what Alciel, at the Devil King's side, had told Libicocco. He had ordered most of the Eight Scarves' forces out of Heavensky, mainly to prevent a large-scale battle with the volunteers set to invade the capital. Such a clash would mean civil war, as well as horrible bloodshed among human and demon—even the emperor might not be spared. Besides, Maou knew from Gabriel that the heavens would be happy as long as Emilia fought and defeated Alciel.

They didn't need things to go that far. And Alciel knew that, which was why he hurriedly negotiated with the Azure Emperor to deploy his troops to the hinterlands. This he did with great success, and in remarkably short order. His under-the-table acting skills had a lot to do with that, although not even Maou knew about that quite yet.

What he did know, however, was that Alciel had a very important reason to take that tactic. A reason why the Great Demon General hesitated to dance exactly to the angels' script—a screenplay that would end with thousands of Efzahan knights and civilians lost and the very empire thrown out of balance.

But that would mean—

"…"

"What?" Emilia asked when she realized Maou was staring at her. He just shook his head. This was something no human should ever be allowed to know. He turned back to his phone.

"I'm sorry," he said, "but I'll have to explain later. Hey, Suzuno? I'll let you handle the nitty-gritty human-world stuff for me. We're kinda busy right now. You worked for the Reconciliation Panel, right? I'm sure you can use that old geezer to your advantage just fine. Later!"

"Ah, Mao—"

His smoke screen in place, Maou put the phone back in his pocket and looked above him.

"Was that all of 'em, Ashiya?"

"I believe so," the demon replied, nodding as he stood up. "The man in the red armor is new to me, though."

"So I let 'em go in Act One, but now it's time for Act Two, huh?"

"Indeed. Some among us are growing impatient of this farce."

The rest of them followed his gaze, faces grave. Amid the howling winds above Heavensky, there were three figures—all people they had seen many times before, no matter how much they hated to.

"Garriel…" came the stony word from Alas Ramus, lost in the wind as she patted Acieth's hair.

✻

Olba, watching Maou and his cohorts from above, had much to be concerned about. This was not at all part of the game plan. He could hear the cries of confusion and terror from the Eight Scarves among his fairly shattered Phaigan Volunteer Force.

The battle, suddenly screeching to a halt. The towering plume of purple light. And now the Hero and Great Demon General, fighting a duel beyond all human comprehension, were all gathered around a lone man, as if having a family reunion before their eyes. The impromptu royal force that had chased the mysterious pair of vehicles all the way into the Cloud Retreat were no less astounded.

Why the Devil King Satan was still in his temporary Japanese form was a mystery to Olba, but there was no way *they* couldn't have picked up on it. His interference wasn't in *their* scenario—but if *they* came onto the scene, not even Satan himself would live to tell the tale.

And just as Olba was trying to reassure himself of that, the exact group he hoped to see appeared from the heavens. The two Malebranche holding him down looked up in awe, as did Emilia and Alciel above. No, nothing was over yet. It just meant that *they* and Emilia had a few more "enemies" to defeat. With *their* strength, they could wipe out everybody in the keep above, wrapping up everything nice and neat.

He tried to call out to them.

"Gabri—"

"How nice to see you in good health, Olba," came the cold, sharpened voice behind him. He knew the voice well—and the cunning of the woman who possessed it. "I had known you were in Japan, but your whereabouts were unknown. Imagine my surprise to find you in Efzahan!"

"Y-you…!"

"But as happy as I am to be reunited with you, my lord, I am even more filled with sadness. Yes, sadness, for my position demands that I question you about your crimes. The apostasy you have carried out in the midst of your dark, dirty scheming, is something I could never allow myself to ignore."

"You," Farfarello said, spying the voice's owner from his vantage point next to Olba. "So you arrived here on those…those 'scooters,' then?"

He nodded at the sight the recently appointed Great Demon General had first seen on the roof of Tokyo's city hall building.

""Crestia Bell…""

Crestia Bell, chief inquisitor of the Church Reconciliation Panel (aka Suzuno Kamazuki, if you asked the gang over in Tokyo), softened her voice.

"That, I am afraid, was not me. I returned from the Western Island just a moment ago. The riders of those vehicles are up there."

"What?"

Bell gave a glance upward, face tightening in spite for just a moment before she composed herself and faced Farfarello.

"Malebranche chieftain! For now, just this once, I deliver upon you an order from Crestia Bell, Great Demon General of the New Devil King's Army."

"Wh-what?!" Barbariccia exclaimed, still out of the loop. "A new general?! Farlo, what is she saying?!"

"Lord Barbariccia," Farfarello replied, "enough."

"B-but…"

"What is your command, my new general?"

"B-Bell, what is the meaning of…?"

She ignored Olba's grunting voice.

"Malebranche chieftain, I command you and your forces to obediently accept everything that will happen from this point forward. Do that, and the Devil King Satan will forgive your abuse of authority and restore you to your original position underneath Camio, Devil Regent and proxy of the Devil King."

"H-human!" Barbariccia blurted out once more. "You know of Lord Camio?!"

Farfarello, for his part, sagely nodded.

"Very well. I will follow every word of your command, Great Demon General."

He looked up, gaze sharpened upon the three figures that faced off against the Devil King, their true master.

"There is no excuse I can make for our foolishness, but it has resulted in betrayal at the hands of Olba and the denizens of heaven. Many are the brethren we have lost as a result. I must accept my punishment for it."

"I am glad you understand, Chieftain. May I ask the same of you, Olba?"

"What are you...?"

If looks could kill, Olba would have just committed first-degree murder. The shadow of a woman he once knew, the faithful agent of the Church who solemnly performed "that which must be done" against the heretics who turned against her religion, was no longer there. Now she was brimming with confidence, and the resolve behind her strength—one backed by a pride he never knew she had—felt all the more invincible now that it was so close by.

"What is the meaning of this? What has happened to you...?"

"What I seek," Bell quietly replied, "remains the same always, Olba: All I wish for is a world where all peoples can walk the path lit by their faith. A faith filled with peace and justice for all. It just so happens I had to travel to another world to obtain the spiritual strength to achieve it."

She looked back up at the confrontation above. If her eyes didn't deceive her, the giant figure in crimson armor was Camael, the man who crushed the final scrap of faith she had in the god she believed in. The unfamiliar man with the Afro was likely Raguel—Maou and Emilia told her about him. But she didn't need a second look at the final angel. The large stature, the cheese-eating grin, the I Love LA T-shirt—it all spelled Gabriel, the guardian angel of the Yesod Sephirah and a man nobody enjoyed seeing crash their party.

✳

"Yo, guys!" Maou brightly grinned. "Glad to see you bunch of third-rate actors finally showed up."

"Ugh." Raguel scowled. "How many times do you have to get in our way?"

"Satan... Satan!!"

And whether Maou was in demon form or not, Camael's shouting indicated he was about ready to spit fiery lava from his mouth.

"You better not expect any mercy this time," Raguel continued. "You may have gotten the better of Camael last time, but we're on Ente Isla now. The atmosphere is filled with an inexhaustible supply of holy power. You have no chance, Devil King."

"Raguel, man, you know you should try actually winning first before you say that. 'Cause you're gonna be pretty embarrassed if it doesn't happen, you know? And you know I'll rub it in your face, too. I'm kinda the demon boss, besides."

"Oh, we'll know real soon how this turns out. It doesn't look like you've got whatever weird strength you beat Camael with, earlier."

Maou didn't take the bait, instead turning his barbs to another target.

"...So, Gabriel. You gettin' in this, too?"

Gabriel, located next to Raguel, crossed his arms and gave a less-than-overjoyed nod.

"Mmm, if that's a yes-or-no question, I guess yes?"

"And I guess I don't have to ask you..."

From the moment he laid eyes upon him, it was clear Camael was intent on tearing Maou limb from limb. He lacked the tri-tipped spear from Sasahata North High, but he knew an archangel could be just as jaw-droppingly strong with his fists.

"We need to keep the peace up in heaven, okay?" Raguel said. "So that's why we gotta exterminate evil demons like you throughout Ente Isla. And that's why we can't have you in our way, Devil King Satan."

Maou gave him an indifferent snort. "Third-rate as always, huh, aren't you guys? Leave that crap to the Hero; she was doin' a much better job at it earlier. You all got walk-on bit parts compared to her, and what're you telling me? 'Exterminate evil demons'? If you wanna rip somebody off here, don't copy her word for word!"

"Here he goes again…"

Emilia rolled her eyes. It wasn't the first time she'd heard this.

"Say what you will, Devil King, but we need that to happen for our plans. And whether Emilia is on your side or not…" Raguel gave Emilia a very un-angelic sneer of disgust, eyes honed to a dim, sharpened edge. "But what next, I ask? Bare your fangs all you want, but you are siding with the Devil King and betraying all mankind in front of the largest audience in the history of this planet. So what next?"

"…"

"Don't forget, now, your father's fields are still controlled by Olba and us. Defy us now, and we'll crush both the Devil King and the father you've only now seen again."

"Huh? Your father's fields?"

Maou spun around toward Emilia. This snippet of info was news to him. Emilia found it impossible to look him in the eye, head hung low as she blushed. To him, she was sure, it must have seemed like handcuffing herself over something that was ultimately insignificant. Her heart sank at the ridicule she expected.

"…Well, whatever."

But it never came. At least, what did come certainly beat "What are you, stupid?"

"We all got different things we value in life. I mean, that's what…" Maou turned toward Raguel, a weary look on his face. "That's what makes this third-class act so fishy to me. How serious even are you guys, anyway? I mean, yeah, he's an incurable sexual predator, but at least Sariel actually worked to make his dreams come true. That's a thousand times better than you guys."

He scrunched his nose and lips together, then hit the palm of one hand with his fist. "So," he hoarsely spat out, "if I can blow you guys out of the sky with one hit, that'll keep you from messing up Emi's fields, right? Wherever they are; I dunno. You think you're up for this, Acieth? Even with Nord how he is?"

When they found Libicocco guarding over Nord in the Cloud
Retreat, Acieth had "transferred" herself from Maou to him. And if
the way she described it was correct, having her new "latent force"
be unconscious would make her own strength take a hit. That, and
she was still crying and blowing snot out of her nose. But she was
still ready for this, a purple aura surrounding her.

"You. The very, ah, hard-looking one."

"Mngh?! Ahh?!"

Acieth casually sidled up to Alciel.

"Maou, with you, throw up very, very much. But with that, it holy
energy at core, so I think, maybe, it works? So can I take?"

Without asking for permission, she then took the kneeling Alciel's
head between her hands and forced him up.

"What?! H-hey! Where are you putting your... Stop this at once!
Have you no shame?! What are you doing?!"

The bold armor that represented the might of the Great Demon
General was now being taken off, piece by piece, with her bare
hands.

"Aah! How could you do such a thing?! After—after all this..."

This was no longer Alciel. It was now Shirou Ashiya shouting and
flailing about. The grace and beauty that every inch of the armor
and cape boasted was being ripped off, torn into little bits by the
Yesod child. The amount of time and money it took to make, and
the dignity it brought the Demon General, made Shirou Ashiya
scream in agony.

"Ooh, I found it!"

After reducing the Demon General to a half-clothed state, Acieth
held her prize in the air. It was a Yesod fragment—the one that Olba
had brought into the demon realms. The one that, in Barbariccia's
hands, had exuded enough power—not holy, but demonic—that it
set off Ciriatto's Crystal Link in the skies above Choshi.

"If I look to you, maybe it work with this one."

"Wh-what are you talking about?!"

Ignoring the dishonorably declothed Demon General, Acieth
turned to Maou, gave him the victory sign, and—her interest in

Alciel now completely gone—gave a quick flip of her feet and zoomed toward him.

"Whoa... What're...?!"

She fell into her arms, their foreheads approaching each other. Despite the intensity of the situation, it still made Emilia blush a little.

"Oh. Right." Maou nodded in relief. "I guess you think so, huh? 'Cause I was thinking I was just being too self-conscious. Guess you couldn't blame me for being wrong."

The moment she heard his reply, the area around them was bathed in a bright, opaque purple light—and inside, his forehead touched Acieth's.

"I think, it only work with head to head. To 'know.'"

Then it activated.

Ensconced in the magic barrier, it was all she could do to keep a grip on her father.

When Emilia finally dared to open her eyes, she was greeted with a bizarre sight. Torrents of purple and black were everywhere—torrents of wind, or light, or darkness, or perhaps sand. But only black, and only purple. The sky that symbolized the greatness and beauty of the capital was painted anew in these two colors, and the voice that echoed from above was low and heavy as it said:

"Damn, do I have some great people on my staff."

Well, perhaps not all that low and heavy.

"I'm amazed you had this fragment with you, Ashiya."

"Oh?"

"Being exposed to demonic force for all that time... Guess that's what made it easy for Acieth to work with me."

"...Heh-heh-heh!"

"?!"

The black and purple currents disappeared, only to reveal Sadao Maou—just as before, in human form and still exuding untold amounts of demonic force.

"Prepare to death, mean crappy angels!"

Then came Acieth Alla, eyes burning red and lips pulled into a vicious sneer.

"Maou! Let's kill!"

"You got it."

With that action-hero one-liner, Acieth gave the demon king a toothy grin. Her teeth seemed to glint a bit as her body instantly transformed into particles of light that took Maou's body in among them.

Emilia watched in wide-eyed surprise. This was exactly how it looked whenever Alas Ramus fused with her. And what happened next was enough to make the jaws of Emilia, Alciel, the three Malebranche chieftains, Olba, and all the Eight Scarves forces on the ground drop.

"…The Better Half…?"

The Hero couldn't believe her own eyes. The sight of it in Maou's hand made her body shake. This was the very one she wielded, the one Alas Ramus had fused with. The only difference from hers was that its blade coursed not with the holy power she enjoyed, but demonic force. But she could tell from the atmosphere surrounding it that this was no pale imitation.

"Another…holy sword…?"

"A-ceth's my liddle sister!"

Amid all the shocked faces, only Alas Ramus looked on in delight, the sheer joy on her face impossible to hide.

"Little sister? That girl? Acieth Alla?"

"Yeh! A-ceth's my liddle sister. The other side of the Yeffod!"

"The other side…"

The description stupefied Emilia. She had never thought too deeply about the name "Better Half" before. She assumed the "Better" part was a reference to how it changed form as she infused it with more holy force. "Half" was, well, part of the name—combined with Emilia's force, the idea went, it finally formed into a whole.

But that wasn't it. "Half" of a sword is just that. An incomplete picture. There had to be another one of the same kind.

"Buh…but this is a *holy* sword! Why is the Devil King…? Why demon energy…?"

"It would seem," Alciel said as he frantically used his own demon energy to repair his battered armor, "that Yesod fragments are not beholden exclusively to the holy side. We have perhaps made one very incorrect assumption about the Sephirah. The sword composed of you and Alas Ramus, and the one composed of my liege and that girl, are not of holy composition at all... Oh, there's supposed to be another button here..."

"Yeffod is a branch that connects life 'n' life. Heart 'n' heart. I was together wif A-ceth. Forever!"

"A branch that connects lives...?"

"Daddy, good luck!!"

Before Emilia could process her words, Alas Ramus started urging Satan on to battle. He responded by twitching his lips and giving Acieth's sword a swing.

"Ngh?!"

"...!"

"Wowwww!"

Just one swipe made all three angels steel themselves. All Maou did was hold his "other" holy sword aloft, and it was enough to make them cower. That was the power it offered—the kind of bottomless power Maou had enjoyed during the pinnacle of his Ente Isla conquest. And it came from a bawling child of the Sephirah and a little pebble Olba decided to bring into the Devil King's realm.

"Right," Maou muttered. "So you're all gonna be outta here in one sec. Then the humans down there can talk all of this out, and you can't put a strip mall on Emi's field or whatever you're planning to do with it. The rest, I'll figure out later."

"What...? Nrrghh...!!!!"

None of them heard the end of Maou's statement. Before he could react, Raguel was suddenly thrust backward by a shock wave that weighed upon him like a sack of elephants.

They had all failed to track Maou's movements. To Gabriel and Camael, it was as though Maou had simply taken over Raguel's position among them. They could tell from the ensuing second shock wave that Maou was moving faster than the speed of sound.

Emilia covered Nord and Alas Ramus in a holy barrier, while Alciel kept himself protected, not daring to risk any more wardrobe malfunctions.

Instinctively, the two remaining angels manifested their weapons— Camael his black-steel spear, Gabriel his Durandal sword—but it couldn't have been more meaningless.

"Satan... Today, you die..."

"H-hey, Camael? I know you don't have chill, but this is kind of a bad scene, man..."

For once in his long, long life, Gabriel actually looked concerned about something. But the hate seemed to ooze out of the slits of Camael's full-face visor, the force of his eyes as sharpened as the tips of his weapon.

"Satan die! Satan die! Satan die! Satan die! Satan die! Satan die! Satan die, die, *die!*"

"...Look, seriously, man, we've never even met."

"Satannnnnnnnnnnnnnn!! Raaahhhh!!"

Camael's spear, thrust forward so quickly it created an air vacuum behind it, was lightly swiped away by Maou like it was made of paper-towel tubes.

"Nnhh?!"

"Ngh."

Seizing the initiative, Maou slashed at Camael to his right, then fired a jet-black blast of energy at Gabriel to his left.

"Sataaaaaaaann!!!"

"Gah!"

The two archangels failed to keep up with the sheer speed of it all. Camael's spear, overpowered by the holy sword, was cleanly split in half at the center, while Gabriel, unable to block the impact, was sent flying just as far as Raguel.

Three downed angels, tossed aside in three different compass directions—and there, eyes burning as red as the moon that hung above him, Maou lorded it over them.

"I'm angry, all right?" he said. "Angry at *you* for tormenting my friends, my staff, my people, and the humans I'm gonna be conquering sooner or later. You will *not* get any mercy from me today!"

"W-wait a minute!"

Emilia hurriedly injected more holy power into her father's barrier to strengthen it. But Maou was moving so quickly, so unpredictably, she feared only hugging the barrier itself would be enough. It was impossible to catch him with the naked eye. Gabriel, as well as the armored angel she had only just met, were doubtlessly fighting with superhuman strength. But now the archangels who had toyed with them so ruthlessly on Earth were at the mercy of a lone figure, Sadao Maou, who wasn't even in his demon form.

The new Better Half sliced through the already-partly-missing Durandal, this time right at the handle—and then it was Maou ripping off armor, Camael's armor, like so much construction paper. Against Raguel, only now recovering from that first blow, Maou didn't even have to use his hands. A bolt of spiritual force from his eyes made part of his Afro vanish.

"Whoa, man, that's going too far— *Ahhhh!!*"

A beam of red light from the tip of the Acieth Better Half struck Gabriel in the shoulder. He spun through the air.

"Satan, Satannn!! Youuuuuuuuuuuuu!!"

Camael, his chestplate destroyed in a single swipe, writhed in pain.

"Holy crap, are you really the Satan Gabe had dancin' around on his hand?!"

And Raguel, whose Afro now looked like a concave jigsaw-puzzle piece, didn't even dare approach Maou. As he himself had once said, perhaps he wasn't cut out for battle.

"Yeah, well, I got my daughter watching me. Don't wanna disappoint her, now do I? Rah!"

"Oooooohh!!"

Maou swung the Better Half at Raguel. It was just a tease; he was too far away to be in range. But the force of the swipe still struck home, slashing at Raguel and leaving countless small scratches across his entire body.

✳

On the ground, silence reigned. Olba, Barbariccia, Farfarello, and all the volunteers were too shocked to even gasp in awe. The events above them were simply impossible to grasp.

And out of all of them, it was almost certainly Olba who was quaking in his boots the most.

"They...they're archangels... How could they be so...?"

He believed with every atom of his brain that if worse came to worst, the archangels would swoop in to save the day for him. They certainly had the strength for it, and Maou at the peak of his powers was, at best, an even match for Emilia. Olba knew that. He had been there.

"...It is almost time, then."

The only coolheaded one among the crowd was, of course, Maou's "friend," Crestia Bell.

"B-Bell, what will happen to all of us?" Olba bellowed, spewing spittle at the composed Church cleric. "These are actual angels! If you pledge your support to the Devil King... You intend to turn traitor to Emilia? To Ente Isla? To the heavens themselves?"

"A surprise to hear such words from your own mouth, Lord Olba."

Bell smiled. She was no longer in the dimension of faith Olba spoke of. She left her position and turned toward the Phaigan volunteers.

"You know there are no such thing as true angels."

"...Wha...?!"

Despite his crimes against the Church, hearing such words from a high-level cleric even made Olba blanch. *What is this girl saying? Does she not see the very beings above her?* He turned his eyes to the three angels. But Bell shook her head.

"Not them," she concluded. "They are mere humans. Humans claiming to be Gabriel, Camael, and Raguel. And if growing wings and possessing great strength makes one an angel, then let me strap on some costume wings from Tokyu Hand and claim my place in heaven! Surely, Olba, you could not believe that the 'angels' sung of in our holy scripture are these people you see before you?"

There was no derisive smirk on Bell's face as she spoke, no look of disgust. She was simply speaking of faith to one who refused to believe she had any.

"The 'angels' we place our faith upon are symbols of the innate goodness within us. Of the standards expected of us in life. We learn of them in our doctrine and scripture, and thus they are ensconced in all our minds. They are not these visitors from afar who wield powerful force. There is no telling how you might have strayed from the path, Lord Olba, but seeing someone I respected so highly be unable to understand something like that saddens me deeply."

Her expression loosened a bit as she watched Olba, before she stiffened it again.

"...Those who serve under the heroic flag of the Eight Scarves, listen and heed my words!"

She called for the knights who surrounded them, still staring dumbstruck at the battle above.

"I understand your confusion and wonderment. But what you see before you is nothing but the pure, unadorned truth: We are now blessed with the presence of two Heroes. And now they each wield their holy swords to once again rid the great empire you love so dearly of the 'devils' that have plagued it anew!"

"Wh-what?!"

"Devils?"

"Two heroes?"

"But...Lady Emilia..."

"It looks like a holy sword, but such power...?"

"That fiend Alciel's the only 'devil' I see here!"

Considering they had been gathered here for the sole purpose of slaying Alciel, the knights were not exactly convinced by Bell's speech.

"Bell, what could you be thinking...?"

Even Olba found himself frustrated at the audacious but ultimately absurd-sounding attempt at restoring order. He had no idea what her motivations were, but someone shouting on her soapbox at a time like this wouldn't attract her any believers at all.

"It is true! That is Alciel, the Great Demon General himself! But it is neither Alciel, nor the Malebranche forces, that has brought this national crisis to the heart of Efzahan. Allow me to prove it to all of you now! Let me introduce to you Archbishop Olba Meiyer, companion to the Hero Emilia…"

"Huh?!"

Olba panicked upon hearing his name. Bell continued, undeterred.

"Sir Albert Ende, another companion…Libicocco, Malebranche chieftain…"

"Gah!"

Bell pointed at two figures nearby—Albert, and the one-armed Malebranche. Their presence was another surprise to Olba—but the third, and greatest surprise, was the person standing next to Albert within a holy barrier. He was small, much smaller than Bell, with his hunched-over back only making him seem shorter. The ornate robe he wore served to make him all the more frail and feeble-looking. There was hardly any majesty to him at all.

But it was still him.

"…And most of all, His Highness, the Azure Emperor of Efzahan, will attest to my words!"

Bell's quiet words struck home with the crowd.

"Y-your Majesty…?!"

The voices quivered even more than when Alciel first appeared, just as the morning sun served to fully illuminate him before the throngs.

"Our leader…"

"The Azure Emperor…!!"

"Our supreme leader!!"

"The emperor!"

"Your Highness!"

"B-bow your heads! All men, bow your heads!!"

The sight of the old man, barely able to stand on his own two feet, shattered whatever high ground the volunteer forces had left. Their knights abandoned their weapons, brought hand and fist together over their chests, and fell to their knees one by one as they showed their fealty to the elderly emperor.

By Alciel's orders, he had been guarded by Libicocco up to the point Maou made his appearance—and by Maou's orders, Libicocco now sent him forward, protected by the barrier Albert conjured, a tiny, frail man who could have been felled by a stiff breeze. He was the Azure Emperor himself, ruler of all the lands claimed by Efzahan across the length and breadth of the Eastern Island.

The august emperor, his blurred eyes and dry, pallid skin weaving a patchwork of wrinkles, glanced at the sky and let out a scratchy sigh.

"Someone," he groaned out. As if electrocuted into life, one of the generals in the top-ranked Regal Jade Scarves battalion sprang to his feet.

"Regal Jade general...what...the woman has told all of us...is the full and unvarnished...truth."

"Y-yes, sire!"

"I was tricked...by the sweet words of those...who called themselves angels...into bringing the Male—ahh, Malebranche here..."

"Yes, sire!" cried the general once more, straining to take in every muted syllable of his ruler. Whether they would come together to form good news or bad wasn't the point. All the Azure Emperor spoke was the truth, and being imparted the truth in such direct fashion would be a highlight of any Eight Scarves officer's career.

"It was all...to build greater Efzahan into...a strong empire...to show the world...the strength of our people..."

"It is the utmost of honors, Your Grace!"

"But...they were of the vulgar sort...the product of the western savages' detestable myths... They abandoned me, and treated Heavensky as their own... They brought my people into war between man and demon... They wounded many of us."

The words that found their way out between the Azure Emperor's labored breathing still managed to retain the ambition, the sheer anger, that had brought him to his post in the first place. They would not let him down now.

"But Al—Alciel...kept me safe...in the Cloud Retreat. He acted to...keep my faithful Knights...of the Eight Scarves...from being forced into…shedding each other's blood. He saved my people, and… and brought us the great heroes from the West. As a strategist…he knows no equal."

This was enough to make even the Eight Scarves begin to stir.

"If…if only…Alciel…was the first dark one…to come to me… perhaps…my power would now extend across all that sees…sees light."

It was a startling confession for the demons on hand to take in. If it had been Alciel who was sent by the angels, not Barbariccia, Ente Isla might be united under the flag of a single ruler by now.

"My…faithful…warriors…of the Eight…Scarves. Do not misjudge your enemy… Gather under the holy swords…and show the heavens…the power…of Efzahan."

There was no way the old man's subdued voice could have reached the ears of all the soldiers on hand. But somehow, everyone in the volunteer force once again bowed down, to a man.

"…I promise you, most respected of emperors, that I, Crestia Bell, chief inquisitor of the Church Reconciliation Panel, as well as my companion, the Archbishop Olba Meiyer, have accepted the sagacity of your words."

"B-Bell, what are—"

"Yooo, Olba! Lookin' good! How long has it been, huh?"

Before Olba had a chance to gripe about his title being used without his permission, Albert turned over custody of the emperor to the Regal Jade general and slapped an arm around Olba's shoulder, as if spotting an old friend at the other end of the bar. He flashed a broad, guileless smile.

"C'mon, we're both deep with the Hero, yeah? Let's work together here! Right?"

He brought his lips to Olba's ear, his voice lowering.

"And I dunno what you were after, but I'd guess it's not in the cards for you now, eh? You could least die with some human dignity in the end."

"A-Alb—"

"Right!" Albert bellowed, holding the struggling Olba down with one thick arm. "Exactly! Now, Inquisitor Bell, tell me: Who should we be focusing on for now? Who's the *real* enemy that threatens the future of Ente Isla?!"

Bell gave him a nod and pointed a single finger upward.

"As the leader of the Church Reconciliation Panel, I hereby lay down my judgment. The true enemies of humankind are the enemies of those who carry the holy swords. The three heretics who dare to claim the title of angels!"

"Keh...heh... Ha-ha-ha-ha-ha..."

Gabriel, arms and legs drained of power and drifting helplessly as Maou held him by his T-shirt, let out a pained laugh.

"S-seriously, this is cruel... I-I leaked so much info to you, can't I get a break?"

"I already *was* going easy on you, you selfish prick. This whole time, you've been treatin' me like a fool, and now it's time you pay me back!"

"Oh... Yeah, true...heh-heh..."

"Look, I'm not gonna kill you, okay? I'm just gonna drag you back to Japan and make you cough up everything you know."

"J-just not so rough, okay...?"

"Sure. Just clear that with *her* first. She's a lot more unforgiving than I am."

"Ooh, yeah, I bet she's a firecracker..."

Their eyes were, predictably, both fixed on Emilia. She was in no position to hear them, but she must have picked up on the vibe, because she lobbed a nasty stare back their way.

"Oof..."

"Sa...ta..."

On the hand opposite the one Maou was using to hoist Gabriel upward, he was holding Raguel and Camael by each of their collars. They groaned in abject discomfort.

It was, in the end, a lopsided victory—far more of one than Maou had anticipated. Raguel and his cohorts were all on Ente Isla, capable of flexing their muscles to the fullest, and not even he could have predicted that the Sephirot's guardian angel would be so…well, disappointing, strength-wise.

"So how 'bout I just ask this for now—like, what's Camael got so bad against me, anyway? I've never seen him before, and frankly, he's freaking me out."

"…Mmm, that's kind of a long stor-eeeee, y'know? And kinda related to what you probably wanna make me cough up the most."

"All right, let's save that for later. Though really, you're one thing, but what should I do with the other two? If I just wanna keep 'em away from their powers, then… Hey, actually, what about Erone? He's from Gevurah, right? Isn't Camael responsible for him?"

"…Yeaaaahhhhh…" Gabriel nodded. It must have just occurred to him, too. "Yeah, you're right. Hey, Camael, what's up with that? If he actually put in an honest day's work, maybe we wouldn't have been pummeled like this, huh?"

"Huh?"

It came as something of a surprise to Maou.

"Wait, so is Camael fused with him like Emi is with Alas Ramus?"

"Not fused, exactly, but…why is Erone—"

"Maou!" Acieth suddenly shouted from within Satan's mind. *"Did you say Erone?!"*

"Eesh, don't scream in my ear like that. Yeah, I did. You know about him?"

"Of course I know! But Erone, I do not feel him here, he couldn't be latent force for him!"

"What?!" Maou exclaimed. Acieth claimed Camael couldn't be Erone's latent force. So the archangel couldn't merge with the fruits of Sephirah?

"Hey, uh, my Yesod just told me Erone isn't here."

"…Wait, what? But he was with us before we came here… Camael, I thought you had him under your control, dude!"

"Under control?!" Acieth shouted again. *"He is so the stupid! We not controlled by anybody! All Sephirah, they work to complete the 'Da'at,' and when the Da'at is done, we are free! The latent force, it is only for temporary! We are jewels that build world! Nobody give the rules to us!"*

"Whoa, Acieth, you're kinda overloading my mind again…"

"Maou! Forget these idiots! Help my sister and her latent force find Erone! Then we go their home and beat all up! Hurry! Hurry! Like, super hurry! Hurry more!"

"Dahh, just chill out! I need to work out a few things first, so let's just—"

"Devil King! Up there!!"

"—get out of here and… Huhhh?!"

By the time Emilia's voice rang out, it was already under way.

"Geh! What is *that* thing?!"

The "thing" that made Gabriel groan in fear was a rift in the clear, sunlit sky that quickly formed into a dark crevice. That was eerie enough in itself, but it also let off no shock wave of force, no sound. The way nobody saw it coming until Emilia warned them about it was the strangest thing of all.

"Uh, D-Devil King," Gabriel stammered, "we'd better get outta here. This is, uh, real bad."

"Huh?"

Maou had never seen him like this before. He thought it was another act, but the emotion in his eyes was not at all Gabriel in his typical state. He was terrorized.

"Th-that's a Gate, but not any normal Gate. It's gonna grab every-one and— Aahhhh!"

"Wh-whoa!"

"Aieeee!"

"Wh-what is the meaning of this?!"

Like a vacuum cleaner going to work on some dust bunnies, the Gate that opened up in the early morning sky began to apply an overpowering suction force upon everyone below it.

"Erng! Wha…what is that?!"

Even Bell, still on the ground, was fighting with everything she had to avoid being picked up. But even relaxing for a moment made it feel like gravity would fail her. Albert and Olba were in the same boat, and the Eight Scarves knights formed a sort of scrum over the emperor to keep him safe, but even that looked dangerously precarious.

"Nh, ah, no…"

There was nothing nearby to latch on to. In a moment, Bell's light frame was almost off of terra firma. She clawed at the air, hoping to find some kind of purchase, but her strength seemed to be totally absent.

"Ah…"

Like a leaf, Bell was tossed into the air…

"Why are you releasing yourself from your duty?"

…only to be stopped by something above her. Bell turned toward the large presence supporting her weight.

"L-Libicocco?!" she shouted.

"After all the resilience you showed me in Japan, you should hardly be flailing about like a child right now."

She had been saved by the very demon who had nearly killed her once before.

"Y-you…"

"I am not being drawn upward."

"What?!"

"And neither are Farlo, nor Barbariccia. Nor my lord Alciel, nor the Devil King… It would seem this Gate can only absorb strong sources of holy force."

"How…?"

She looked around. Albert and Olba were still fighting the force applied to them, but it didn't seem to be affecting the Eight Scarves knights nearly as much.

Then she looked up.

"Whoooooooooa, whoa whoa whoa! Goddamn it!!"

There he saw Maou, still holding on to the angels in both hands, looking about ready to get sucked in with them.

Not even Gabriel could resist this attractive force—"Garghghrhhh, ow, ow, I am *soooo deaaddddd*" were his exact words—and being stretched between the Gate pulling him up and Maou pulling him down was starting to exact its toll on his T-shirt's integrity.

"Nooooooooo!!"

"E-Emi!"

The Gate seemed to be affecting Emilia just as badly.

"Keep… Keep fighting it, Emilia! You call yourself a Hero?!"

"That…that kind of doesn't apply to this…!!"

"Enough struggling! Do you wish for me to slash you with my claws?!"

"Don't…don't worry about me! Just save my father…"

"Bah! Why do I have to protect someone like Emilia's father?!"

It took the combined efforts of Alciel and Farfarello to keep Emilia stationary. But just like Bell and Gabriel, she was unable to control her own body. Nord, covered by the holy-magic barrier, was not as affected, but the Gate seemed to be sucking in his barrier instead, forcing Barbariccia to dogpile on top of him.

"Dammit, Gabriel! What the hell?! What's going on?! …Agh!!"

Before he could find an answer, the left hand Maou used to hold the collars of the two angels slipped in the howling wind.

"Whoa, wait! …Shit!!"

All it took was a single moment's inattention. The results sent the unresponsive Raguel and Camael high into the air, through the crack in the sky, and out of sight.

"That… Hey, Gabriel!!"

Maou managed to reel in Gabriel by his clothing. Figuring he'd lose his grip before long, he grabbed him by the neck and elbows from behind in a wrestling hold, pulling him down with all his might.

"Arrrgghh!"

"What's happening?! It's going for the strongest holy-force users first!!"

"I…I can't…breathe…"

"Hey!! Gabri—"

"Maou! Up there!"

It was then that Acieth, sounding more nervous and more resentful than ever before, made herself known. Even as he tried to steady his grip on Gabriel, the voice made Maou crane his head upward.

"That…"

Inside the gate, he could see a small dot. A human-shaped one. It was not that large; maybe about as tall as Urushihara or Sariel. But it was much wider around than either of them, thanks to the ball-shaped head and bulbous outline that made it look almost like a plush animal.

Maou had seen a silhouette akin to this on TV not long ago. Something even a child in Japan would recognize. And it wore the type of clothing that Maou would never expect to see in a time or place like this.

"Is that…a space suit?"

The figure inside the Gate was dressed in what could only be described as astronaut gear. The opaque visor kept its face completely hidden from Maou's vantage point, but somehow, he could tell this visitor was trying to tell him something.

Then:

"Aaaaaaaaaaaaaaaaaaahhhhhhhhhhhhhh!!"

Acieth, inside Maou's mind, let out a tormented scream.

"A-Acieth, what is it?!"

"Nh… Nraaahhhahhh!!"

The anguish continued unabated.

"What's wrong, Alas Ramus?! Are you okay?!"

Then Maou heard the one thing he didn't want to hear: Emilia herself shouting in pain. The moment he heard Acieth's yelp, he knew the theory he had in mind was true all along.

"Emi! What is it?! Is Alas Ramus…"

"I-I don't know! She's in some kind of pain…"

"Dammit… Why is this happening? Acieth! Get it together!"

"Ma… Maou… I can't… It bad hurts… Aaaaahhhh!!"

"Alas Ramus! Alas Ramus!!"

It happened to Maou's and Emi's body at the same time: particles of purple light leaked out from them both, then shot toward the crevice.

"Mommy! Mommy, ow! Owwww!!"

"Maou… My body…! Aaaahhhhhhhh!!"

"Alas Ramus!"

"Acieth! Ahh, dammit! Gabriel! What is this? Who *is* that guy?!"

"You're…choking me… It's how it works… Us archangels… Who d'you think…we take our orders from…?"

"Your orders…?!"

Why hadn't it occurred to him before now? These people calling themselves "angels" in front of him—apart from the Heavenly Regiment, they all treated themselves as equals. Sariel, Gabriel, Camael, Raguel—whether they were the guardian of this or the judge of that, they all held these impossibly lofty titles, but they were all of the same rank as far as heaven was concerned.

But they said it themselves—orders from above. Their "missions." And who gave those to them? It could only be one thing.

"Something like that should never exist. Not on this world."

The moment the thought came to Maou's mind, the pull of the Gate above Heavensky suddenly disappeared. The force working upon Emilia and Gabriel, without warning, suddenly returned them to the rule of gravity.

"Agh!!"

The recoil force thus applied to Gabriel's neck and head was enough to finally knock him out. But Maou had other matters in mind.

"A-Acieth? You okay?!"

"Alas Ramus! Hang in there!"

The moment the force disappeared, the particles streaming out from Maou and Emilia stopped. The pain that tormented Acieth seemed to be gone, and the same applied to Alas Ramus, given by how Emilia was calling frantically for her, one hand to her chest.

That came as a relief, but when he looked up at the gate again, he was greeted by a shocking sight that made everything that came before seem like child's play.

"Waaaagghhh?!"

"Whaaaaaal?!"

"Gaahhhhh?!"

The moment Alciel, Farfarello, and Barbariccia saw what Maou did, they let out screams that sounded like something from another world.

"Wha—wha—whaaaaaaat?!"

"L-Libicocco, what is it?!"

Even on the ground, Bell was surprised at Libicocco descending into fear right after saving her life. But it was Maou, most of all, who couldn't believe the sight facing him. It was so preposterous, it made him want to scream.

In a way, it was even more enigmatic than the astronaut, and even more terrifying. The broad hat, with a peacock feather stuck in it that seemed to gently lilt in the deafening whirlwind was a blindingly, shockingly bright shade of purple. The hair that peeked out from under it curled in almost noble fashion, contributing elegance even as the similarly covered silk dress clashed against it. One arm, carrying a handbag whose strap teemed with embroidered jewels, sported a bracelet that seemed to draw a springlike spiral around her wrist, and the manicured nails struck fear into Maou's heart at a single glance.

The body was like a barrel of TNT, the legs like two gigantic cannons, and the white-enamel stiletto heels couldn't have possibly sustained the weight of the whole thing. It was a portrait of female elegance beyond human comprehension—enough to make the rising sun want to retreat back east for a while—but for innumerable reasons, a portrait that belonged nowhere near here.

It was Miki Shiba, landlord of Villa Rosa Sasazuka, a wooden apartment building several million miles away from here.

"Ms.…Ms.…Ms. *Shibaaaaaaaa*?" came Maou's confused scream.

With the gentle breeziness she always bore, Shiba turned her head (despite having no visible neck to work with) toward Maou and gave a refined nod.

"Well, hello there, Mr. Maou! It's been quite a while. I do apologize if I am interrupting anything."

"Oh, uh…not interrupt, exactly, but…um…"

"Chiho Sasaki was kind enough to inform me of your affairs. Normally I would never allow any of this, mind you, but apparently Amane's been revealing quite a bit to all of you…"

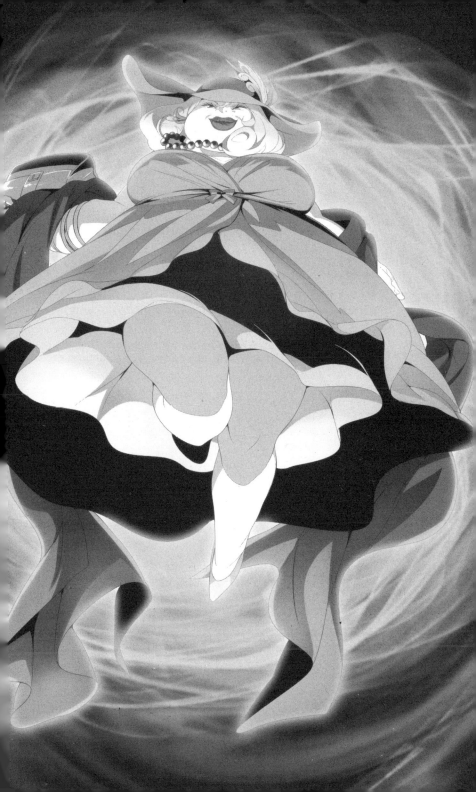

She paused to look at Emilia. They had spoken before, if only once, and Maou could see the massive question mark written on her face.

"That," Shiba continued, "and I could hardly leave the children using you and that lady as latent forces *entirely* to their own devices."

"L-latent...?"

Why would Shiba know a term they had only heard from Acieth before?

"I suppose," she replied, "I've not grown quite heartless enough to leave my younger brothers and sisters fully in the lurch."

Then, with a smile that had the force of a nuclear blast on all it was directed toward, she turned to the Gate in the sky.

"And I do hope you will all retire from this scene for now," she said to the astronaut inside. "I imagine you understand how unwise it would be to defy me?"

It was hard to say whether the figure heard it, but the astronaut briskly turned its back to the rest of them. Then:

"Ah..."

As everyone of them looked on, the Gate vanished, with no sound, no lead-up, and no warning. All that remained was the sky, the two moons, and the thoroughly wrecked Heavensky Keep below them.

"Is... Is that it?" Emilia whispered as every man, every demon, and every angel slowly regained their senses.

"Oh, no, nothing is over yet," Miki Shiba said, still high above them. "In fact, one could say it has hardly even started yet. Chiho Sasaki did not lead me to believe things were in quite as much of a disarray as they evidently are. Yes, quite a disarray indeed, over on this world..."

"Ms....Ms. Shiba, could you at least tell me—"

"Ohhh no, no, no! That's 'Mikitty' to you."

"Oh, o-okay..."

Anything spoken through those thick, firm, glossy lips, covered in a blazing shade of crimson that even put Camael's armor to shame, was impossible to disagree with.

"Mr. Maou—and all of you too: Mr. Ashiya, Ms. Kamazuki, Ms.

Yusa—I would like to request that all of you make your way back to Japan. And you, too, you lovable guy! We can discuss matters after that."

Shiba's "lovable guy" was apparently Gabriel—the archangel who, after a pitched battle, had been half-strangled by Maou as he tried to keep him from being sucked into the Gate. Somehow, Maou didn't think he would find the experience too non-horrifying. For once, he had some sympathy for the man.

"B-but wait a minute!" Emilia shouted. "We can't just leave things like they are here…"

It was a world-changing day. The angels who schemed against Efzahan and the Malebranche were defeated, the mysterious Gate a thing of the past, but that alone would not stop the disorder. There were countless healthy Malebranche down there, and the Eight Scarves forces would hardly just salute to Alciel as he traipsed back to Japan. Whether or not the angels or demons were pulling the strings, Efzahan was still officially in a state of war against the entire rest of the world.

"Oh, no?" Shiba countered. "It hardly has anything to do with me."

"B-but…" Emilia turned toward the thousands of eyes watching her from below. The throng was nervous. They didn't know what to do with themselves. Should they keep fighting? If so, against whom? The old Emilia Justina probably would have an inspirational word or two for them to live by. But now she knew all too well how selfish she was. She only cared about fighting for herself, and nothing she could say in her current state would move the minds of anyone. And whether or not he had a Holy Sword, she doubted the Devil Lord would ever pinch-hit for her.

Then, just as suddenly as the big one from before, a small tear opened up right next to Bell on the ground.

"Ah…"

"Mnh!"

It portended a Gate, albeit a tiny one. Everyone steeled themselves, preparing for the worst.

They shouldn't have bothered.

"Oof! …Oooh, boooy, talk about a big messss…"

"Very much so. I was not expecting this."

Two people stepped out of the Gate—two people Emilia knew very well.

"E-Eme?!"

One was Emeralda Etuva, Saint Aile court sorceress and a figure who should've been under trial for betraying her religion at the moment. The other:

"And…General Rumack?!"

Emilia's voice went a notch higher at the even more unexpected visitor. Hazel Rumack, about ten years older than the Hero and dressed in the beautiful ceremonial armor she wore for diplomatic missions, winced at the chaotic scene greeting her through the Gate, but gave Emilia high above an exaggerated wave nonetheless. The Eight Scarves around them, now reassured the gale force from the previous Gate was gone, were busily attending to the Azure Emperor's safety.

And looking at all of it from above, Miki Shiba whispered:

"The people of this world can handle their own business."

"Everyonnne! Please, do not fight any longerrr! That is a formal request from Emeralda Etuuuva and Albert Ende! Hold yer fiiiire, y'all!"

"The emperor seeks an armistice as well! Hold yourselves for a moment! If you do not stop, then by the name of the Hero Emilia I will strike you down!"

Before any further action could be taken, Emeralda and Albert had stepped up to quell the masses, each in their own trademark fashion.

"…All of you," Bell shouted, "come down here!"

Maou, Alciel, and Emilia exchanged glances.

"You may go ahead," Shiba said. "You do have enough time for that. In the meantime, I'll take this man, and then…"

"Uh?"

"Eh?"

Shiba twitched her finger a little. The limp Gabriel was instantly whisked out of Maou's arms, to hang in the air like a breaded fish filet tossed into the fryer. Then Maou and Emilia began to faintly glow, and in the next instant, a gaunt-looking Alas Ramus and Acieth appeared before then.

"I will take care of these children for you. After all, Mr. Maou, you would be quite a bother to those on the ground in your current state, would you not?"

Regardless of what the two "latent forces" thought about it, being relieved of their Yesod fragments so easily only deepened their awe at Shiba's mysterious powers. Maou gave Emilia a look, and then, holding back his demonic force as much as possible, settled down to earth.

At the time, they still had no idea why Alas Ramus and Acieth simply manifested in space like that.

❋

"You certainly have been busyyy, haven't you? Heavensky Keep is just an utter shaaambles."

"Completely!"

Emeralda and Suzuno were the first to greet Maou and Emilia.

"You knooow, this may shock the world even more than when the Devil King's Army destroyed Isla Centurrrum."

"Uh, sorry," the Devil King awkwardly offered.

But there were still a few things he didn't quite understand.

"Hey, but, Emeralda, weren't you summoned to religious court or something? What're you doing around here?"

"R-religious court?!" Emilia blurted out. This was news to her, but the easygoing Emeralda eyed Bell instead.

"Welll, Bell and Rumack helped me ooooout."

"Suzuno and General Rumack?"

"Oh, it was hardly any great labor," said the general in the ceremonial armor. "We just prodded at the sewer rats lurking around the nation a little."

"Rumack found out I was on triiial for apostasy, and she went all the way from the Central Connntinent to the capital for me."

"And why wouldn't I? What kind of empire does this to a woman, is what I ask you? Emeralda would normally help herself out of that predicament a bit more easily. I figured Pippin had to be involved, and boy, was I right!"

"Aw, you make it sound like I'm the bad guy," Emeralda protested.

Rumack shrugged. "Well, weren't you?"

"I was nooot!"

Emeralda puffed out his cheeks in dissatisfaction. No one stepped up to defend her.

"Plus, I could hardly rescue Emeralda this fast by myself. It was Sir Albert and Inquisitor Bell's support that did the trick."

"Yeah, about that," Maou interrupted. "Suzuno, you went all the way to the Western Island and back? How?"

As far as he could remember, Suzuno and Albert were about to sneak into the capital half a day ago. What were they doing with Rumack and Emeralda over there?

"We failed to infiltrate the Cloud Retreat...and Gabriel sent us back to Saint Aile."

"Oh, right, Libicocco said you guys got tossed somewhere..." Maou gave another glance at Gabriel, still bobbing in the sky under Shiba's force.

"I honestly thought," Suzuno said, "we had no chance of coming back. But Emeralda was in the capital. With her support and the angel's feather pen, I thought we still had some hope."

"I tell youuu, when Bell and Al and Rumack storrrmed into the courtroom I was in, I thought I was halluuucinating!"

"The courtroom... Ah!"

The reminder helped Maou recall Crestia Bell's position in the Church.

"Indeed. Placing one of Saint Aile's most important figures—a companion to the Hero, no less—on trial was a massive under-taking. One that should never have been attempted without the approval of the leader of the Reconciliation Panel. The only one ranked above me is Archbishop Robertio, current head of the Panel. It puzzled me, the question of who gave this sort of permission so recklessly."

A trial for apostasy, or refusal to obey one's religion, involved a judge determining what, if any, teaching of the Church the accused had turned their backs to. That was the sole jurisdiction of the Reconciliation Panel—or the Council of Inquisitors, as it used to be called.

"I tell you," Suzuno said, "when General Pippin Magnus caught sight of me as he reclined in his witness's chair, he practically fell off!"

"Right," Albert added. "And while she was putting an end to the trial, Ms. Rumack tied Pippin down long enough to get all the trial evidence back out in the open."

This retelling of the epic legal battle, taking place halfway across the world from this one, was starting to strike Emilia dumb.

"I didn't have my guaaard down or anything, but, oooh, having that maggot Pippin do me in… It made me stew in my own juuuices, for sure. Didn't it?"

Emeralda suddenly turned toward Olba. Only the traitor himself and the people surrounding him knew it, but between the disappeared Raguel and Camael, the defeated Gabriel, and the Malebranche now firmly back on Maou and Alciel's side, Olba had no true ally left in this city. His body shook, too battered to stand up, and Emeralda stared at it like a snake.

"Wh-what?!"

"Oh, stop playing duuumb. You sure were buuusy, weren't you, you outcaaast?"

Even the bald tonsure on top of Olba's head was white as a sheet.

"You bribed the bishops in the walled city of Cassius into ignoring you, you built inroads with that worm Pippin and his gang, and you let them take over the area around Sloane, diiidn't you? I'm sure that rat Pippin just *loooved* the payoffs you were giving him, nooo?"

"That…"

"And when I started sniiiffing around Sloane, you locked me in the capital for that stupid triiial. You were on cloud niiine, weren't you? And then Bell came stomping in, and *swoosh!* went Rumack's rapier, and you wouldn't believe all the dirrrt we found!"

"Ah...ah..."

"Rumack brought it all into the triiial, and Bell gave the Church judge an eeearful of scary legalese, and with that, Archbishop Cervantes came all the way from Sankt Ignoreido through the Stairs to Heavennn, and then he went down on one knee and asked for my trial to be annulled! And why wouldn't heee? Not only was there clear evidence of what the missing Olba had donnne, we even had evidence for the Cassius bishop's corruption!"

Emeralda seemed to be tormenting the now ghostlike Olba with every word.

"The Church knights and imperial guards around Sloane are all on our side now. And I can't help but wonderrr, what were you ever trying to do with my good friend's family hooome?"

"E-Eme?!" Emilia blurted out. "Is that...?"

Emeralda and Rumack were in full control of the territory around Sloane. And that meant only one thing.

"Emilia," Emeralda gently replied. "We failed you at your time of need, and you had to go through so much. But it's okay now. Your father's fields are under the direct protection of the Holy Magic Administrative Institute now."

Emilia covered her face with both hands and let out a soft sigh. It was a sound from the heart—a sound of relief, of happiness, of regret, and of hope.

"Olba Meiyer," Emeralda continued, boldly, with the full force of her Saint Aile court-magician title behind her. "You have deceived our people, denigrated the teachings of the Church, put countless thousands across the world in danger, and dragged the good name of the Hero in the mud. For that, you must have penance—and it is not a crime you can atone for simply with your life."

Olba was sprawled on the ground, lifelessly, as he listened. Now, finally, his sins were exposed to all the world.

"But if there is even a shred of human decency left in your heart...

If you have the will to speak the truth about this darkness covering Ente Isla, the Holy Empire of Saint Aile will give you the opportunity to wipe away your sin. Olba, your foolish dreams end here!"

"Gnh..."

Albert lifted Olba up by the arms, restraining him. He offered no resistance. Realizing his will was completely broken, Emeralda sighed deeply.

"Ahhh, this is such a loooad upon me..."

Rumack sighed at the display. "See, that's what I mean when I say you're a bad guy. So..." Hardening her expression, she turned back to the former Phaigan Volunteer Force knights, all carefully eyeing her now.

"Members of the Eight Scarves... My name is Hazel Rumack, the Western Island's representative in the Federated Order of the Five Continents. I have arrived in search of an audience with the Azure Emperor."

This was not at all how normal diplomacy worked. Having a top official hop in via a Gate and demand top-level talks with the Big Guy would spark an international incident in itself, but trying to talk to the emperor without an appointment went even beyond that. It was downright *rude*.

But it worked.

"Let us...hear out this one," came the raspy voice of the Azure Emperor as he stepped out from the knights—a figure who wouldn't even be seen by most visitors without an advance message from known nobility.

"This has been a trial...for all of us. Underneath the azure sky, both I...and you, remain human beings...at heart."

"I am grateful for the compliment, Your Majesty."

Rumack bowed her head, as per the custom in Efzahan. Emeralda, herself a high official from Saint Aile, followed her lead.

"Your Grace, on behalf of the Federated Order of the Five Continents, I am here to formally ask you to lay down the spears of war for good."

"...Hmm."

"The tragedy that struck Heavensky today could very well prove to be a mere taste of the tragedy all of Ente Isla is facing now. The scars of the Devil King Army's rampage remain fresh upon us. If human must battle human again, it could lead to a yet darker, more final disaster for all of us. It might mark an end to the grand history your nation has built for itself, and I do not believe, Sire, that is what you seek."

"...Hmm."

"I beseech you, Your Grace, to send a representative to sign an armistice with the Federated Order. It will take only a moment of your, and his, time, but it will help all of us—North, South, East, West—enjoy the peace we enjoyed in pre–Devil King's Army days for at least that one moment longer."

Listening to Rumack's rhetoric, Emilia gave Maou next to her a glance.

"...Huh?"

Then she asked herself why she did it. She knew that answer to that, of course; instead, she was wondering whether Maou cared about how Rumack placed responsibility for all the world's wars on the Devil King's Army.

Ente Isla before the demon invasion was hardly a utopia where people stood hand in hand in beaming harmony. Tensions ran deep under the surface between the world's superpowers, with all-out war between smaller nations an all-too-common occurrence. The specter of civil war was fresh on the minds of both Efzahan and Haruun on the Southern Island.

Rumack was speaking in diplomatic terms, of course, and nobody else had to interpret her literally that way. But, to Emilia, it made her realize that she was actually mulling over Maou's feelings. It threw her a bit.

On the other hand, the true target of Rumack's request gave a far less muddled response.

"...Very well. The declaration of war...from earlier...was the product of my...my unworthiness. The commander of...the Regal Azure Scarves...shall be sent hence."

"...It pleases me greatly to hear, my lord."

Rumack bowed deeply in appreciation.

Once the impromptu conference was over, the emperor, guarded by a squad of Eight Scarves soldiers from Phaigan, returned to his domicile in the bit of Heavensky Keep that managed to avoid the most catastrophic of damage. Once they saw him off, Emeralda and Rumack ran up to Emilia.

"You have liiittle to worry about nowww, I would say."

"Yes. And while you may not believe it at this point, Emilia, I feel the people of Ente Isla are slowly, but surely, sensing the weight you've borne for them all this time."

"Eme... Rumack..."

"We want you to fight for yourselllf from now on, Emilia. Al and I will give you our utmost supporrrt, too."

"...All right. Thanks."

Emilia attempted a nod, but the events of the day were too overwhelming, and she ended up hugging her friend instead.

Emeralda must have known it the whole time—the Hero never fought for anybody except herself. But Emilia was always there for her, regardless. She wanted to repay that friendship, no matter what it took.

Rumack gave them a smile, then hardened her glare on another man nearby—the one with enough demonic force locked inside him to level an entire continent.

"I must admit, I am surprised to hear you are the Devil King who laid waste to Ente Isla. Normally, the idea of chatting with you like this would seem ridiculous to me."

"Yeah, don't I know."

"But...oddly enough, it appears that to Emeralda, Albert, and Emilia most of all, you are an indispensable part of their lives. Without the strength you and Inquisitor Bell lent to us, we could never have rescued Emeralda, revealed Olba's crimes, and brought Efzahan back to the Federated Order's bargaining table again. We could never let bygones be bygones, and it is up to us to judge you demons for your sins as well, someday...but, for now and now alone, I thank you."

Alciel looked perplexed at the general's light nod, Bell meekly bowing her head. Maou, on the other hand, grunted at it.

"C'mon. You know I'm the Devil King and these're demons, right? Maybe I blew it last time, but I'm not giving up on conquering Ente Isla yet. Get all namby-pamby on me, and I'll make you regret it sometime."

"Let us pray that 'sometime' never comes," Rumack countered with a bold smile. Then her eyes turned to the Malebranche chieftains behind Maou. "Them, meanwhile... It would not at all be in our best interests to let them go back to this 'Japan' I hear of. If you are not willing to do something about the Malebranche, then I'm afraid hostilities will have to begin immediately."

"Yeah, yeah, yeah. You know I've been itching to order these guys back into my realm."

Maou winced as he spoke—

"Hup!"

—then, as if opening a bedroom window, he opened a Gate right next to Rumack.

"Barbariccia?"

"...My liege."

"Ciriatto's already over there, yeah? I really hope you've had enough of this crap by now. Try to lie low for a change, all right?"

"...Yes, my liege."

"Your Demonic Highness!" Farfarello said, falling to one knee.

"Mmm?"

"Everything has happened as you said it would. Please, forgive us for our ignorance."

"Ooh, glad to see I'm getting a little respect for a change. Can you get the rest of the Malebranche outta here, too? No stragglers."

"Yes, sir!"

"...You," Libicocco mumbled, staring at Bell. "I know not what your intentions are...but try not to get yourself killed."

"Ah, never in my wildest dreams did I imagine a Malebranche

worrying about my health." Bell rolled her eyes, although she didn't seem too offended to the others. "I pray that the next time we meet, we fight with words, not swords."

"Nonsense. You humans and your ridiculous ramblings..."

"Indeed. And I feel that I understand the demons less than I ever have before."

It was a sight that would have been unthinkable just two years ago. And one that, until today, would have been unthinkable anywhere except Room 201 of Villa Rosa Sasazuka in Japan. But here it was, right on Ente Isla. Humans and demons, talking. And seeing this unthinkable act take place before her eyes, Emilia couldn't help but bite down hard on her lip.

Upon Barbariccia and Farfarello's command, the Malebranche left in Heavensky assembled near the ruined keep. As Rumack looked on warily—still not used to such huge numbers of demons acting in orderly fashion around her—the New Devil King's Army returned home, via the Gate the real Devil King provided for them.

"Hey...Devil King..."

"Mm?"

Emilia spoke up behind Maou—this time as the swordless, Cloth of the Dispeller–less Emi Yusa.

"I know I said earlier I need to apologize to you about something, but...um."

"The Malebranche?"

"...Yeah, I..."

Slowly, Emi explained the events that had happened to her: her arrival on Ente Isla, her discovery that her father's land was still fertile, and how she led the volunteer force to kill innocent Malebranche chiefs for the sake of a few simple acres of wheat. All in the utmost detail, with no embellishments. Maou listened to every word of it, not interrupting once.

"So," she concluded, "I guess I really have no right to condemn you for—"

"Oh, who cares? I sure don't. Stop acting so stupid."

"What?"

"Maybe this sounds cold, but really, I couldn't give two shits any longer."

"You couldn't...? Aren't the Malebranche under your command?"

"Yeah, but I told Farfarello to recall his forces, like, eight million times since he showed up in Japan. Barbariccia and the other chieftains didn't listen to me. They misread the situation, and they died for it. All there is to it."

"...B-but..."

"Why is *that* shaking you, of all the damn things? If you're saying you killed demons from the start just for the sake of yourself, how's that any different?"

"...!"

He was right. But it didn't mean it would be easy for Emi to grapple with this in her heart quite yet. Maou, perhaps realizing her ambivalence, let out a contrived sigh and shook his head.

"I mean, you're the Hero, and I'm the Devil King who made you that way, and I don't see the need to keep arguing over that. Because ultimately, none of this changes a thing between you and me."

Maou chose this moment to finally turn toward her. Why, even now, did Emi flinch away? Why was it so hard to look him in the eye? Whatever the answer, it was nothing Maou cared about.

"Like, if there's anything that's changed, it's that I said you were one of my Demon Generals, huh?"

"Wha...!"

Emi's face shot upward. Being called such in public wasn't the issue. It was the events surrounding that appointment—events that even now made her blush.

"That... You... I mean, that was all *your* doing! I never said I would accept it or—"

"Yeah, see? That's what I mean. It was *my* doing. Come on, Emi. You know you've got more important people to apologize to. Don't tell me you forgot about *that*, too?"

His expression suddenly turned glum.

"I mean, hell, by now, you're probably gonna have to serve as Chi and Rika's slave."

Emi's mouth opened a little.

"Chi was bawling her eyes out every day you didn't come back, and thanks to that wacky Idea Link you threw Rika Suzuki's way, she had to see Gabriel whisk Ashiya away. That kinda sucked, you know."

"Oh...um..."

"And I already got Chi's birthday present, too, all right? But I'm sure you didn't get anything, as if Chi wasn't pissed at you enough already."

"......Ooh."

The shock of the truth, coupled with what her shallow behavior had done to her friends, stunned Emi into a groaning silence.

"Man, seriously, what is wrong with you lately? You sure you didn't get food poisoning or something?"

Emi was too busy bashfully fidgeting with her hands to give a coherent reply. Maou scowled, but then gave her a pat on the shoulder. "Well," he said, "I guess that's how tough it was on you, huh? So when we get home, you can apologize, and you can tell 'em everything from square one. They're your friends, right? They'll understand."

"......Yeah," Emi said with a nod, bringing a hand to the arm on her shoulder.

✳

The contact came rather suddenly.

Chiho, on her way home from school, had just put her schoolbag back on the desk in her room when the phone rang. Lunging at it, she looked at the screen—and instantly shot out of the room, everything in her heart bursting out at once.

"Chiho?! Are you going out again?!"

Her mother was a tad surprised to see her daughter zoom out the door right after trudging back in, but Chiho's heart had no capacity left to deal with that. She was on the street now, and with a single sense of mission, she ran across Sasazuka as dusk settled down upon it.

The way took her down the 100 Trees Shopping Arcade, full of people picking up dinner or returning home from work or school. It

made forward progress a little dicey at times, but Chiho darted and
dodged her way through them as fast as she could.

And, of course, she hit a red light just before the rail station.

"Ughh!!"

So she went two steps at a time up the pedestrian bridge that
ran under the Shuto Expressway that rings Tokyo. Traversing the
entirety of it would take about as long as simply waiting for a green,
but Chiho still ran on, undeterred. In fact, she heard the tone indicating the green light behind her just as she coursed past the guard-
rail behind the Sasazuka rail station.

The area was, as usual, littered with parked bicycles, but Chiho
didn't care. She was on Bosatsu Street now, gently curving upward
as it went. She went straight along the irrigation channel that lined
it, crisscrossing along a few alleyways as she did.

In just a few seconds, her target was in sight—a battered old
two-floor apartment. A place dearer to Chiho than almost anything.
A place where the people she cared about gathered.

"Ah!"

And as she ran, she could see it—a familiar-looking light in the
backyard. Wiping the sweat from her eyes, she sped the rest of the
way, careened past the VILLA ROSA SASAZUKA sign, and burst into
the backyard.

"Maou!!!!"

She shouted the name she had seen on her phone screen, the soles
of her shoes crunching down on the grass. It hadn't been that long
ago since she helped weed the backyard, but those weeds were right
back where they used to be. The people there, however, were more
interested in something else.

"Ooh, Chi, that was fast."

"Ah."

"Ooh!"

"Hmm?"

"Ooh, Chiho!"

"Chi-Sis!!"

It was a packed house. Some were calm and composed; some looked exhausted; some like they had just gotten back from a day at the office; and some unconscious while riding on other people's backs. And one of them, her face a little hidden away, was a little softer-voiced than the rest.

"…Chiho."

"Yusa…"

At that moment, a waterfall of tears began to flow from Chiho's eyes; she couldn't hold them back. Chiho let impulse guide her as she made one more leap forward and into the other girl's arms.

"Yusaaaaaa! I'm so haaaaappyyyyyy!!"

"Ch-Chiho…"

"I-I-I was soooo worried! Really, really worried! I thought, oh, what if I never got to see, *snif*, nhh…*ennhhhhh*…"

"Chiho… Thanks… I'm sorry, I'm sorry I made you worry…!"

Emi gingerly stroked Chiho's shoulders as she cried into her chest.

"Hi, Chi-Sis! …*Waph!*"

"Alas Ramus…"

Feeling a small hand tug at her skirt, Chiho looked down at the young face before her and gasped. In a moment, she was kneeling and held the child in her arms.

"Thank heavens you're okay…! Just… This is just so wonderful…!"

"Ahh… Chi-Sis, don't cry…"

"*Wehhhhh…*"

Alas Ramus, oddly eager to play the older-sister figure ever since she regrouped with Acieth, patted Chiho's hair.

After taking a few moments to compose herself, Chiho took another look at the assembled group. Realizing Ashiya was carrying Gabriel on his back, her eyes opened wide—and seeing an unfamiliar man on Maou's back, she turned to Emi again.

"Yusa! Yusa, is this…?"

"Uh-huh," Emi said, nodding a bit bashfully. "I'll introduce you once he wakes up. It's my dad."

"Yusa!!!!"

Overcome with emotion, she let go of Alas Ramus and grabbed Emi yet again.

"Wow, what a tearjerker, huh?"

With a snarky jab, Amane opened up the window to Room 202 and stuck her head outside.

"Nice to see you're okay, Ashiya. I gave her the message for ya!"

"My thanks to you." Shirou Ashiya, clad in his UniClo outfit with the stretched-out collar instead of his Great Demon General armor, gave Amane a wry smile.

"Did anything happen while we were gone, Amane?" asked Suzuno, still in her robes. Amane laughed and motioned with her chin.

"Um, duh? If Aunt Mikitty came to visit you guys, you just know some stuff went down over here, too."

"Amane?"

Shiba, who returned to the apartment with the others, had just given Amane what, in Maou's mind, seemed like a pretty harsh lecture. "Well," the landlord sniffed, "we could never house Ms. Yusa's father in Mr. Maou's or Ms. Kamazuki's rooms, and I hardly think we are in any shape to send them to a hospital or Ms. Yusa's apartment. So let me open up Room 101 for the time being. You can put your father in there, Ms. Yusa, and I think you should find it suitably clean."

"Oh, um, thank you," Emi said, appreciating the gesture even as Chiho still clung to her.

"Mr. Ashiya, if I could trouble you to carry that wonderful young man over to my house for me? I need to fetch the key to Room 101 anyway, so I'll gladly go with you."

"C-certainly," Ashiya said, his face just as strained as Maou's. Assorted anxieties crossed both of their minds. What tragic fate awaited Gabriel inside Shiba's private residence? And after all that work to return to Sasazuka safely, if Ashiya blundered into Shiba's house, would he ever come back alive?

"Right," Maou said, gauging the crowd as he rebalanced Nord on his back. "Let's go into my place. Our stuff is coming pretty soon, and this is getting kinda heavy, so..."

"Your...stuff?" the similarly encumbered Emi asked.

"Oh, assorted things," Suzuno cryptically replied with a grin. "I suppose we will owe Emeralda another favor soon." Then, realizing something, she turned to Amane. "By the way, how is Lucifer doing?"

For Amane, the question seemed awkward somehow. She turned her eyes to the side. "Yeah, um, Urushihara... Well, thanks to that 'stuff' I mentioned, he's in the hospital right now."

"What? He's still not discharged yet?"

Amane's statement was shocking enough. Chiho's reaction to it—the fact she already knew this bit of news—only made everyone more uncomfortable.

"Eesh," Maou sighed. "And I was hoping things were a bit more chill back here. Well, at least we're over the hump."

He flashed a smile to Chiho, still latched on to Emi and shedding tears.

"Glad to be back, Chi."

Chi replied with a world-beating smile of her own.

"Maou," she chirped, "Yusa, Alas Ramus, Ashiya, Suzuno, Acieth...

"Welcome back!!!!"

EPILOGUE

Nord's unconsciousness—more of a coma, really—lasted far longer than Emi had envisioned. It had already been a week after Gabriel took him and Ashiya from Villa Rosa Sasazuka and two days since he'd been brought back, but Nord Justina was still in such a weakened state that he showed no sign of waking.

Maou knew the man had spent some length of time living in Japan, but without any ID on him or any idea where he lived, he couldn't take him to a doctor for treatment. He tried asking Acieth, but the response—"Umm, Mitaka?"—was a little too broad to be allowed by the national health insurance system. Regardless, Suzuno's estimation was that he'd escape mortal danger as long as he woke up within three days, so for the time being, he was safe and resting in Room 101 of Shiba's apartment building.

Emi, for her part, had returned to her own apartment in Eifukucho just long enough to make sure the electricity worked. Apart from that, and a quick outing to furnish Room 101 with a futon and the other bare essentials, she had been holding vigil by her father's side.

In terms of people recuperating at the moment, Urushihara was a more present worry. Amane was being weirdly tight-lipped about it, but judging by the hints Chiho dropped, his hospitalization had a lot to do with Shiba, their landlord. Exactly how—and for that matter, what hospital he was admitted to—was still a total secret.

Once back in Japan, Ashiya was naturally frantic about how they would pay for Nord's medical bills. But, really, their little jaunt to Ente Isla had already given them a litany of questions to ponder. Questions they'd all have to tackle, one at a time, and hopefully with Shiba's cooperation.

Meanwhile, despite the unintentional wringer Maou had put him through while in Devil King form, Gabriel was miraculously still alive. Shiba was housing him at her place, claiming it was still far more touch-and-go with him than Nord. Maou was eager to start grilling them for information, but just imagining the sorts of dreadful horrors waiting inside her place made his hair stand on end. The silence from Ashiya, the only demon to actually step into the house, only stoked his fears further.

As his anxieties ballooned in his mind, Suzuno, back in her usual kimono, rang his doorbell and came in.

"Devil King, may I have a moment with you?"

Despite the grandiose airs she presented as a Church cleric on her home planet, it was clear she wouldn't be back here without the immense strength of Emeralda and Rumack. Archbishop Olba's betrayal, and the collusion between Saint Aile's royal force and the Church, would be more than enough to topple the power balance in the religion's topmost echelons. But having it all exposed by Crestia Bell, who (by words or by force) was the highest-ranked of Church reformers, showed many observers that the Church was now doing its best to heal itself.

That allowed it to escape the worst of consequences. It also meant that Crestia Bell now held life-and-death power over the entire Church. She knew, in fine detail, all about the darker side of its operations, and she was now deeply linked with the empire of Saint Aile—itself linked to the religion strictly through faith and goodwill, not through bribery. Many were those among the Eight Scarves who lauded Bell as another "Heroic companion," to be ranked alongside Emeralda Etuva and Albert Ende, and anyone who dared impede her now would face the wrath of the surviving Church bureaucracy.

Suzuno, for her part, had no interest in conducting a purge of the Church. To her, protecting the faith came first, although when she shut down Emeralda's trial, she made sure Archbishop Cervantes was aware that mercy should not be given to those who twisted the faith for their own purposes. According to Emeralda, when

Archbishop Robertio heard news of this, it was enough to make him fall to the floor in terror.

To sum it all up, it was safe to say that Suzuno—or Crestia Bell—was de facto the most powerful official in all of the Church. One whose efforts to rescue Emilia and save the world in Olba's place gave her more freedom to act in Ente Isla than almost anybody else.

"I told Chiho when I would be conferring with Shiba, and she texted back to say she would join us."

"Oh, that?" Maou reached for his phone. "She texted me, too."

"Indeed, I imagine she sent it to both of us. But I wanted to ask you: Have you noticed Chiho acting strange as of late?"

"Strange?" That crying fit when they first came back was certainly a sight to see, but it didn't seem too out of character in Maou's eyes. "I dunno, I guess she doesn't use as many emojis as she used to? Not that I mind, but…"

The phone was now out of his pocket, and it was still in just as many pieces as it had been inside the Cloud Retreat.

"Would you consider a new handset already? If you plug that in to charge it, you might electrocute yourself."

"Oh, sure, if you're payin'. I'm counting on someone else to cover that, but…you know, it'd be mean to hit her up right now…"

He pointed down at the floor.

"Ah," Suzuno said. "Well, indeed, there are Chiho's texts to consider, but I had another concern."

"Oh?"

"The day we went back, it seemed to me that…perhaps, for just a moment, Chiho was scared of something. Or sad about something, you could say."

"You think so?"

This took Maou aback. To him, Chiho was displaying nothing but pure joy at their return.

"Yes. But I am not entirely convinced, so I wanted to ask you. I wondered, has she discussed anything with you? Or have you done something thoughtless yet again to offend her?"

"Uh, hey…"

"Can you provide a yes-or-no answer for a change, please?"

"Man, you've been really needling me on that lately…"

Maou was sure it wasn't his imagination. For a while now, Suzuno had been sticking her nose into his and Chiho's relationship quite a bit more than she ever did before. He had no idea what he wanted from her, but either way, it made for a lot of uncomfortable moments whenever Ashiya was around, including now.

"Well, all joking aside…"

"That didn't sound like a joke to me!"

"Emilia has asked me to pick up a few things, but it is a tad too much for me to carry by myself. Can you come with me?"

"Huh?" Maou groaned. "Why're you asking me?"

"You do not have to act so peevish about it," Suzuno replied, looking a tad hurt.

"N-no," Maou said, shaking his head, "I just mean, if it's for Emi, I can't help but react like that sometimes…"

"You told me you needed to buy a thank-you gift for the people you swapped shifts with, no? I simply thought you might like some company. You don't have to snap at me."

"What nonsense is this, Bell?"

"Hmm?" Suzuno gave Ashiya an honestly confused look.

"Never in a moment would you think of doing anything together with my liege before now. Can you blame him for being confused?"

"Is…is that it, you think?"

Suzuno took a step back, as if Ashiya's point physically pained her. But just as she did, everyone's attention was distracted by the front door opening behind her. There was somebody on the other side.

"…Oh!"

Rika Suzuki, feeling the eyes of three people upon her, fidgeted nervously.

Emi awoke to the sound of the Room 101 doorbell. Rubbing her eyes, she realized she had dozed off in a seated position.

Her refusal to sleep for a moment as she cared for Nord had

brought her exhaustion to its peak. It was funny—she fought against an otherworldly overlord for over ten hours on Ente Isla, but simply staying awake for longer than twenty-four hours made her feel half-dead inside. She looked at the clock; it had jumped half an hour in her absence.

The doorbell rang again. It was probably Suzuno, back from the errands she asked of her.

"Oh, sorry, Bell. Just a second." Emi brushed her bangs away from her face. "Thanks for carting all that heavy stuff over for—"

The sight of the person on the other side when she opened the door made her stop mid-sentence.

"Hey. Long time no see."

For someone she hadn't seen in a month, it was a markedly short greeting. It came with a plastic bag that Rika now offered to her.

"Rika…"

Emi paused, hesitating to take the bag for a moment.

"Come on, this is heavy."

"Oh, sorry…"

She hurriedly grabbed it. Then she just stood there, wincing and trying to find the right words, not bothering to check the bag's contents.

"Uh, um, Rika…"

"I figured I better tell you what's up, so I asked Suzuno if I could get this stuff for you instead. It was just a little over three thousand yen, so I'll give you the receipt later."

"Oh… Um, so, Rika…"

"One sec. There's something I wanna say to you first. I've got some good news and some bad news—which one d'you want first? I kinda wanted to tell you myself, so…"

Now she was acting just like she always did. Emi still wasn't sure how to react.

"Uhhmm…maybe the bad news first?"

The old TV-show logic seemed worth trying.

"Okay. Well, sorry, but they fired you. The floor leader tried to hold out for you, and me and Maki did our best to cover when we could…but if you go silent for a month, there's not a lot we can do."

"Oh… No, I guess not."

She tried to take it stoically, but the "bad news" was a lot worse than she'd anticipated. She was a veteran of life in Japan, and in that workplace, for a while now. Even if she couldn't reveal the whole truth, being barred from returning to a community she treated dearly took a surprising toll on her heart. In some ways, it was worse than that moment her will to go on as Hero was crushed. She supposed, just like then, that she deserved it. All the shallow lies.

"So, the good news… Could you put that bag down for a minute?"

"Oh, uh, sure…yeah." Emi put the bag on the floor and looked back at Rika. Her Japanese friend gave her a cynical smile and looked her right in the eye.

"I'm gonna give you the chance, right now, to decide what you want me to call you…Emilia Justina."

"…" Emi felt her heart tighten. "R-Rika… I…"

Her eyes burned; her lips shook. But she couldn't cry. Crying in front of Rika, in front of her best friend in this world and a woman she had constantly lied to all this time, would be the height of cowardice. But Rika was quick to observe the change in her.

"Whoa, no crying! That's not fair. I had to go through some really scary stuff, thanks to you. You should be letting me cry instead! Which I did! Like, a lot!"

"…You're right."

"But if I could cut to the chase a little, if there's anything I want an apology for, that's really about the only thing, actually."

"…Huh?"

"Yeah, it was a huge surprise and all. I mean, I thought maybe you were born outside of Japan, but outside of Earth? And you're some hero with Superman-style powers? And you've got a name as highfalutin as 'Emilia Justina'?"

"Superman-style…"

"But you know what? If I was a guy and we were married or something, we'd probably have a ton of emotional baggage to deal with… but thankfully, we're not. I'm a girl, and we're friends."

Emi was too distressed to notice that the logic Rika was using didn't strictly apply to their relationship. Rika was a woman, and her feelings were for another man. For just a moment, the Hero's friend looked up at Room 201 above, with longing eyes, and it wholly escaped Emi's attention.

"Wh-what do you…?"

"…Oh? Well, how about this? I live in Takadanobaba right now, but you know my folks're in Kobe, right? We talked a little about that."

"…Yeah."

"Did I ever tell you about how I got picked to compete in the National Sports Festival in swimming?"

"Y-you did? The nationals?! No way!"

The National Sports Festival of Japan was the largest athletic competition in the entire country—a sort of Japan-exclusive Olympics. They didn't just let any old high schooler join in.

"Yeah, way. I got weeded out pretty quickly, but still. Also, back in middle school, everyone kept calling me Rikappe. I mean, Rikappe? Does the 'pe' sound ever work for a girl's nickname, I ask you?"

Rika laughed at herself, then grabbed the stunned Emi by her hand.

"You see what I mean? Unless you really go out and do it, you never know much about your friends' past at all. With you, the only difference is that you've got a more colorful résumé than I do."

"…Rika…"

"The important thing to me is that we're still comfortable enough with each other to talk a bunch of crap, to stop by the café after work… Well, maybe *that's* not gonna happen for a bit, but still… You know, that's all I really need from my friends. Anything beyond that, it's kind of a bonus."

"Yeah…"

"So I'm not asking you to, like, write a thousand words about your life and hand it in tomorrow or anything. But if you feel like talking about it later, then let's just sit down and do it, okay?"

"Okay…okay."

"Whoa, whoa! No crying! That's my only rule!"

"Okay…!!"

"Oh, brother. Your dad still isn't awake, right? Save that for your big tearful reunion later on, okay? Ugh, I swear, if he sees you for the first time in years like this, he's gonna disown you. Maou as Devil King is one thing, but I'm starting to wonder if you were ever a Hero at all!"

It grew impossible to hold back. Rika held Emi as the would-be Hero's shoulders shook.

"Anyway, keep it up. Hope your dad gets well soon."

"Okay!!"

"…Look, I'll let it slide on the tears, but could you at least wipe your nose? You're seriously starting to annoy me."

She let Emi put her head on her shoulder, gently patting it as Emi sobbed uncontrollably.

"So what d'you want me to call you? Emi like before? Or Emilia like Suzuno does?"

"If you…*snif*…called me Emilia, I'd feel weird…"

Rika gave a sly grin at the thin voice. She gave her a pat on the back, then flashed a smile at her.

"Great! So Emilia, then."

"Huhh?!"

"Emilia, Emilia… Yeah, I like that. It's cool. Thanks a bunch, Emilia!"

"R-Rika, wait, I…"

"And *you* can call me Rikappe if you want."

"That…that's not the issue! R-Rika, please, just stick to…"

"Ooh, if you look at me like that, it just makes me wanna bully you more. Hey, Emi—I mean Emilia—what were you even doing on Ente-whatever over the past month? I kinda want to hear more about you, Emi. Emilia. Same thing."

"See? You aren't used to it at all."

Rika seemed intent on this new game. It was all so silly that Emi couldn't help but laugh through the tears.

"But that was your only job, wasn't it, Emilia? You're gonna have to find a new one before too long, or else you're gonna have trouble taking care of your dad. And it's you taking care of Alas Ramus, too, right?"

"Oh, um..."

Thinking about it, losing a job that paid her 1,700 yen an hour full-time was, for someone living in Tokyo, a pretty major blow. She had a bit of savings to rely on, but if she didn't find something equivalent to that soon, she'd have trouble covering the rent in Eifukucho in short order.

Right now, even if her father was back to perfect health, going back to Ente Isla wasn't an option—at least, not an immediate one. She owed Maou for messing up his license exam, to say nothing of the expenses incurred during the Ente Isla trip, and she promised to pay Emeralda back in some way for transporting them all back to Earth. She had it coming for what she did, perhaps, but things were looking pretty cruel for her.

"You know, Maou and Chiho said that MgRonald's facing a killer employee crunch with the new delivery system and all. Why don't you try applying? And while you're at it, just move into this apartment here. It looks nice and cheap, and at least your neighbors know what's up with you. That'd be easier, right?"

Rika's suggestions might have been based on sound logic and reality, but looking back at her life, it wasn't exactly something Emi was ready to accept.

"I, um... I probably have to start considering that a lot more than before, yeah...but I think both of those are gonna be worst-case scenarios for me..."

"Oh, sure, it's up to you to figure out the details. Just try not to box yourself into a corner, okay, Emilia?"

"Yeah... No, but please, no more Emilia..."

It still sounded horribly awkward to Emi. She tried to figure out how to dissuade Rika from this new habit she was attempting to foster.

Before she could, she was interrupted.

"Emi...lia..."

It was a soft groan, but it still thundered across the room. Emi and Rika exchanged glances.

"E-Emi, I think...I think that was him!"

"Y-yeah, um… Here, come in and sit down somewhere…"

"Forget about me! Hurry!"

Flurried by this turn of events, Emi and Rika sat down next to Nord, lying on his futon. His face winced, as if he was having a nightmare, but this was the most they had gotten from him in the past day.

"Father… Father?"

Emi used one of the wet tissues Rika bought for her to wipe the sweat off his forehead.

"Keep calling for him, Emi!" Rika tried her best to keep her voice down. "C'mon, Dad, Emilia's right here! Open your eyes!"

"…Ooh."

""!!""

They both heard the voice from his lips. Against Emi's eardrums, it sounded just a tad higher than the one in her memory. But it was still good enough.

"<Father…can you hear me?>"

"Oop, more of that moonspeak, huh?"

"<Father… Please, wake up. I have so much I want to talk about.>"

"Hey, your dad knows Japanese, too, right? Heyyy! Anybody there? We got Emilia here! Wake up!"

"Nnn…gh…"

"<Father, you and I can live together. You never lied to me. You said we could live together again someday. Well, I'm here now, Father. I'm here…>"

"<Emi…lia…?>"

"<I… I'm back for you…!>"

Emi and Rika watched as the recumbent Nord opened his eyes—squintingly, but clearly revealing the life they held inside. He addressed Emi in his still-halting voice.

"Whoa, he's awake, Emi! I'm gonna go tell Maou and everyone, okay? Helloooo? Suzuno? Maou! Ashiya!!"

Something about Rika's echoing shouts as she stormed out the door made Nord shut his eyes again for a moment. It must have helped stimulate his consciousness.

His voice was still almost a whisper, but already he was strong enough to sit up from his futon. Emi hurriedly put an arm under him for support. There, in a faraway world, the two stared at each other—a father who used to be a tad younger, a daughter who used to be far, far smaller.

It was Nord who smiled first.

"<Ah, Emilia... Am I dreaming...?>"

"<No... No, you're not...>"

Did I always cry all the time like this? Emi didn't bother to wipe away the unrelenting flood.

"<Father... Father...!>"

On that long-ago day, too, when she was younger, she held her father like this. The tears she shed then were tears of separation, of desperation. But now the tears flowing down Emi's cheeks were illuminated by the light of Earth's sun filtered through the window. Warmly, they shone and basked in the light of hope.

EXTRA CHAPTER

The news of the destruction of Heavensky Keep, the shining symbol of the capital of Efzahan, shot across all of Ente Isla in an instant. Soon, the whole world's focus was on the events in Efzahan, and on the smoldering rebellion that loomed ever larger on the island's eastern side.

The most pressing order of business was to regroup the Eight Scarves forces scattered across the empire and assuage the frazzled nerves of its people—both in the farmlands and in political circles. The organizers of the Phaigan Volunteer Force were the main people responsible for this—and with their walking papers provided by the Azure Emperor himself, a figure they'd be lucky to see even once in their military careers, morale was at an all-time high.

However, there were voices of concern echoing across the land—and with the Malebranche gone, they were growing louder. Their main worries: After declaring war on the world, how would the Federated Order of the Five Continents seek to punish them during their negotiations? Could the Azure Emperor live for much longer? And did he still retain the capacity to lead his people?

As Heavensky, a city once compared to the deep blue sky itself, found itself in a state of frenzied reconstruction, the emperor himself heard of these whispers. His hearing had not failed him yet—but even as the ravages of age sent him reeling, his eyes shone with the unrelenting light of ambition, like a blazing beast seeking its prey.

"He…is a masterful strategist… A masterful commander…"

Recalling his conversation with the overpoweringly strong Great Demon General several days before, the Azure Emperor Hu Shun-Ien bared his yellowed, half-missing teeth as he cracked a sinister grin.

"What we need...is a great nation...ruling the four seas, the five lands...and the one sky."

"He" was now on the same stage as the emperor.

Let him keep dancing, as long as I am still alive, and let him seize the future.

"To cement my legacy...and make the glories of Efazahan eternal..."

His eyes, the eyes of resolve and ambition, were focused on places and events situated far beyond.

"Perhaps it is best, to open the way ahead to someone...not of humankind."

THE AUTHOR, THE AFTERWORD, AND YOU!

I'm sure that all of us, whenever life has us down in the morning, has thought about how great it'd be if a meteor landed on our school, or if our office building exploded into a million pieces.

We feel that way when we've got a specific reason for our depression—an upcoming final exam, a disagreeable coworker—or even if there's nothing particularly wrong. Maybe we just get sick of the same old routine, and the gap in our minds between ideals and reality starts driving us crazy. We look back at it all, and we seriously say to ourselves, "Wonder if there are any meteors around..."

It's not as though people like that honestly want the world to end. They're just looking for some catastrophe that would let them toss away everything weighing them down and head to Hawaii for a bit. Unfortunately, life has a way of not allowing that. No matter how heavy and plodding things are, no matter how much you just want to give up and run away, it's hard to just shove it all in the trash. You wind up doing your thing, time passes, and then things work out good, or bad, or whatever—but since you can't run away or trash it, you do what you can to mold everything in a way that looks nice. Or at least I do.

There aren't a lot of people out there who can decide on something from a certain point, then proceed straight for it, over all obstacles, without any distractions or moments of self-doubt. If we were all like that, this world wouldn't work at all.

The people in this volume are the same way. They're trying to push forward; they're finding themselves lost; they're up against the wall; the road they were taking turns out to be a gigantic trapdoor. But they struggle through it, and now, at the fork they've run into, they're steeling their resolve and trying to pick a way.

Like I wrote in the previous volume's afterword, it's a new stage in the *Devil Is a Part-Timer!* story. And pegging that new stage right on a nice round number like Volume 10, while a total coincidence, both feels great and makes me feel ready to tackle the future in earnest, from Volume 11 onward.

I hope I'll see you there. Until then!!